The Ultimate Read-Aloud Resource

2nd Edition

LESTER L. LAMINACK

Making Every Moment Intentional and Instructional With Best Friend Books

Credits

Text and illustrations from THE RECESS QUEEN by Alexis O'Neill, illustrated by Laura Huliska-Beith. Text copyright © 2002 by Alexis O'Neill. Illustrations copyright © 2002 by Laura Huliska-Beith. Used by permission of Scholastic Inc.

Text and illustrations from POLAR BEARS by Gail Gibbons. Copyright © 2001 by Gail Gibbons. Used by permission of Holiday House Publishing, Inc.

Text and illustrations from SNOW DAY! by Lester L. Laminack, illustrated by Adam Gustavson. Text copyright © 2007 by Lester L. Laminack. Illustrations copyright © 2007 by Adam Gustavson. Used by permission of Peachtree Publishing Company Inc.

OWEN by Kevin Henkes. Copyright © 1993 by Kevin Henkes. Published by Scholastic Inc. by arrangement with HarperCollins Children's Books, a division of HarperCollins Publishers.

CROW CALL by Lois Lowry, illustrated by Bagram Ibatoulline. Text copyright © 2009 by Lois Lowry. Illustrations copyright © 2009 Bagram Ibatoulline. Published by Scholastic Inc.

SHARK LADY by Jess Keating, illustrated by Marta Álvarez Miguéns. Text copyright © 2017 by Jess Keating. Illustrations copyright © 2017 by Marta Álvarez Miguéns. Published by Scholastic Inc. by arrangement with Sourcebooks, Inc.

SPIDERS by Gail Gibbons. Copyright © 1993 by Gail Gibbons. Published by Scholastic Inc. by arrangement with Holiday House Publishing, Inc.

THE KING OF BEES by Lester L. Laminack, illustrated by Jim LaMarche. Text copyright © 2018 by Lester L. Laminack. Illustrations copyright © 2018 by Jim LaMarche. Published by Peachtree Publishing Company Inc.

All rights reserved.

Publisher/content editor: Lois Bridges
Editorial director: Sarah Longhi
Editor-in-Chief: Raymond Coutu
Development/production editor: Danny Miller
Senior editor: Shelley Griffin
Assistant editor: Molly Bradley
Editorial assistant: Sean Cavanagh
Cover designer: Kyle Kirkup
Cover/interior photographer: Bob Leverone
Interior designer: Maria Lilja

ISBN-13: 978-1-338-59494-2
ISBN-10: 1-338-59494-X

2 3 4 5 6 7 8 9 10   40   28 27 26 25 24 23 22 21 20 19

♻ Text pages printed on 10% PCW recycled paper.

Scholastic Inc., 557 Broadway, New York, NY 10012

For teachers and librarians
who understand
the importance and power
of reading aloud:

You ignite the passion.

For the authors and illustrators
of children's books:

You provide the fuel
that feeds the passion.

For young readers and writers:

You will change the world
through your passion.

Videos

Contents

Acknowledgments

Every book is the result of the efforts of many people. My name goes on the cover, but there are many people who worked tirelessly to make this happen.

First, my Scholastic team: I am ever grateful to Lois Bridges, dear friend, staunch advocate, and insightful editor. Thank you for always seeing more in me than I see in myself. Ray Coutu, you have been a friend across many years and your insights with this project have been invaluable. You are a treasure. Sarah Longhi, I have come to deeply appreciate your keen insights and the calm you bring to the table. Shelley Griffin, I am grateful for your guidance and your joy, Molly Bradley, thank you for being ever ready and for pulling together the loose threads, and Sean Cavanagh, I appreciate your enthusiasm and patience. Danny Miller, it has been a pleasure to craft my thoughts knowing they would be passing by your watchful eyes before making an appearance in the world. Brian LaRossa, Tom Martinez, and Maria Lilja, what a pleasure it has been to brainstorm and banter as you work your magic with design.

And then …

I am always under the influence of the rhythm, the cadence, and the power of the voice of Mrs. Hand, the librarian who brought books to life for me. Reba Wadsworth, sister-friend, you have been a rock as I have found my footing through some tough times in life. You are always ready to listen and bounce ideas with me. I am grateful to the administration and faculty of the many schools I have had the pleasure of working with as these ideas have emerged. You have been instrumental in pushing me toward clarity. I am grateful to my dear friends at Shaner Elementary, Topeka, Kansas, for your trust, your questions, and your willingness to try something new. And I am especially grateful to Buffy Fowler and the team at Francine Delaney New School for Children in Asheville, North Carolina, for your unending willingness to partner with me when I have new ideas to explore.

And finally …

Steve, with you my light is brighter.

Welcome, Readers

Welcome, my fellow educators, to an exploration of the art and purpose of reading aloud. Please join me in an effort to make every experience with books intentional, instructional, and like a relationship with a best friend. Join me in an effort to bring read-aloud back to a place of prominence in the lives of children. As you'll discover, the benefits are innumerable.

The interactive read-aloud is multifaceted. It lends itself to both extended chapter books as well as short text such as poetry, magazine articles, and short stories—and it accomplishes multiple, essential instructional goals simultaneously, including:

- Drawing *all* students into the text
- Capturing the interest of disengaged readers
- Expanding students' reading horizons by exposing them to new books, authors, and genres
- Furnishing background information
- Refining students' understanding of *text*—genre, format, literary elements, text structures, and features
- Promoting inquiry
- Promoting conversations using literary language
- Teaching essential strategic reading actions
- Encouraging students to view topics from multiple perspectives
- Improving listening comprehension
- Building academic vocabulary
- Deepening comprehension
- Modeling all aspects of thinking, talking, and writing about reading
- Developing insights into what writers do to support readers
- Demonstrating fluent reading
- Building an intellectual classroom community of readers
- Introducing and modeling collaborative conversations
- Addressing the requirements of higher standards
- Fostering a lifelong love of reading

Jim Flanagan is a fifth-grade teacher at a residential school in Philadelphia that serves primarily children of color from high-poverty neighborhoods. Jim knows well the benefits of the read-aloud because he begins every school morning with a 30-minute session. He explains what the read-aloud means to him and his students:

> A daily read-aloud in every classroom is the place to start reclaiming conversation. When we assemble together in our classroom as a school family, our family dinner is the read-aloud. Each morning, I greet all the kids as they walk in the room and gather around the big table by the windows. If it's bright enough outside, we keep the fluorescent lights off and just use the natural light and a few lamps to warm the pile of books in front of me and read.
>
> Most days the group discussion is insightful, poignant, humorous, and tender. You lay a foundation of interesting background knowledge and compelling stories, and the connections are made in a natural way. Exposing the students to so much, touching on so many topics, locations, and ideas, something always captures every child's interest. You pique their curiosity and expose them to the broad range of what the world offers. There is ample opportunity for the kids to share during the read-aloud, just like there is in an authentic conversation. The teacher guides the conversation and makes sure everyone is engaged and respectful, and that the kids participate and stay engaged. We share and learn about each other in ways we would otherwise never know—and that builds trust, which, in turn, builds love and respect.

Literature, language, and love—this is what a Best Friends interactive read-aloud offers, and you can't beat that!

When Books Become Best Friends

"That was the beginning of a lifelong journey in which books would shape and change me, making me who I was to become."

—CHARLES M. BLOW, *NEW YORK TIMES* OP-ED COLUMNIST

As I share read-alouds with both children and teachers, I take great pleasure in bringing a book to life through the use of voice, facial expressions, and body language. The merits of the experience and the sheer pleasure of bonding with children over a book seem obvious. In fact, reading aloud to children seems as natural as inhaling and exhaling.

Yet I have heard countless teachers express the need to justify time spent on read-aloud experiences in the instructional day. So in this book I hope to reveal the gift it can be in the lives of children and how the books that you read aloud can become Best Friend Books.

What Is a Best Friend Book?

Think about one of your best friends. Reflect on how you met and how your friendship developed. Even if you had an immediate connection, it is likely that your connection deepened over time—through shared experiences, common interests, earned trust, mutual respect, and a growing sense of knowing you can depend upon each other when things get difficult.

**SPOTLIGHT ON
LESTER VIDEO**

**Introduction to
Best Friend Books**

scholastic.com/URAResources

We have many friends and acquaintances, but our "best friends" are a treasure. We know and count on them in ways that transcend our other relationships.

A Best Friend Book (BFB) will be similar. You may feel an immediate connection to it—but it will take time and repeated visits for you to recognize the depth of what it has to offer. It is likely that your first visit will be connecting with the story line, the characters, and their actions in fiction, and with the content, the presentation, the topic, and the focus in nonfiction. That must prove worthy of your attention; it must offer something of substance that will leave you thinking and wanting to revisit. More visits will likely result in small delights and discoveries along the way:

THE TURN OF A PHRASE

This can best be described as an artful or unexpected way of saying something. For example, one might say, "That gives my nightmares nightmares" versus "That's creepy."

Author Jill Esbaum uses an interesting turn of a phrase in her book *Honey Bees*: "She sips the runny nectar through her straw-like tongue and stores it in a special, just-for-honey tummy."

THE USE OF SPECIFIC, CONCRETE NOUNS

Specific, concrete nouns zero in to help the reader gain greater clarity. For example, the writer may say, "I sat on the porch in a metal chair." Now consider how the more specific concrete noun brings even greater clarity in this example: "I sat on the porch in a folding *aluminum rocker*."

In *Prowling the Deep: Exploring the Hidden World of Ocean Predators*, Pamela S. Turner uses specific concrete nouns to provide an example: "More than 90 percent of all large fish, such as sharks, swordfish, and bluefin tuna, are gone."

WELL-CHOSEN, PRECISE VERBS

Precise or vivid verbs provide more specificity in the writing and give the reader a more precise image of what is happening. For example, the writer may say, "Sam *walked* three blocks to the store." Now consider how the more precise, vivid verbs that follow evoke a better sense of how Sam feels on his trip to the store: "Sam [*waltzed* or *skipped* or *sprinted* or *trudged*] three blocks to the store."

Matthew Rake, author of *Real-Life Monsters: Scaly, Slippery Creatures*, uses precise verbs to describe the behaviors of 10 fierce reptiles: "Male water monitors wrestle…they stand up on their hind legs and grapple. Each lizard grips its opponent with its forelegs and uses its claws to rake vivid pink gashes in its rival's back."

THE DEVELOPMENT OF A CHARACTER

Writers develop and reveal characters in a number of ways. For example, the narrator can simply tell you: "Marcus was a large boy for his age, almost a head taller than any kid in kindergarten. His face was sprinkled with freckles, and he had a cowlick above his left eye that made his hair spike up despite his mother's fondness for hair gel." The writer may also develop the character slowly, revealing personality and attributes through the character's actions/reactions, thoughts, or dialogue. In addition, we may come to know a character by listening in on the dialogue of other characters.

In nonfiction, writers devote their attention to developing the topic or building a persuasive argument. Characters are typically not the focus unless the text is a biographical or historical piece that features a person.

THE ARTFUL USE OF DESCRIPTION

Description helps the reader create a sense of things, a sensory awareness. Artful description is a well-placed detail that spotlights or assigns importance to an object, person, place, or action. For example, a writer may say, "Alice poured her morning coffee in her favorite cup and read the paper." But if that cup is of great importance and will have some significant role later in the story, you may find the writer drawing your attention toward the cup: "Alice took the cup from the cabinet and held it just a moment. The inside was stained from years of morning coffee. She ran her thumb over the chip on the rim where her grandfather had nicked it on the edge of the counter in his last days at home. Though she had seen it thousands of times, the image of Bugs Bunny always made her chuckle."

Both fiction and nonfiction authors use rich and robust description to help their readers make meaning. Consider this lead from *A Butterfly Is Patient* by Dianna Hutts Aston: "It begins as an egg beneath an umbrella of leaves, protected from rain, hidden from creatures that might harm it… until the caterpillar inside chews free from its egg-casing, tiny, wingless, hungry to grow."

THE BALANCE OF DIALOGUE AND NARRATIVE

Think of the narrator in a story telling you everything from beginning to end. It can work. But the use of dialogue along with narrative gives the reader insight into the personality of the character. Dialogue can provide bits of the backstory or reveal plans for the future. A story told only through dialogue would read like a script for a play with no stage directions. Balance between the narrative and the dialogue of characters results in a more robust reading experience.

THE ARC OF THE STORY IN FICTION

Story moves through a series of events or scenes in a logical sequence. The most common way to think of a story arc is to move from the initiating event to rising action/tension, toward the climax, to falling action, and ending with a conclusion. You can explore this further in the diagram on page 73.

THE DEVELOPMENT OF AN ARGUMENT

Story can present opportunities to explore an argument. In these situations, we want to notice the character's stance on the topic. We want to be able to search back through the story and find examples in actions, reactions, thought, and dialogue to support the assertion. For example, let's assume two characters are playing in the park and they find a jacket near the swings. One character tries it on and decides to keep it, declaring "finders keepers." The other character insists they take the jacket to the lost and found because some kid is going to get in trouble for losing that jacket. In nonfiction we are likely to see the writer use details, statistics, numbers, and references to research to support a claim or assertion when making an argument.

WELL-PLACED, SPECIFIC TEXT STRUCTURES TO ENGAGE THE READER AND EXECUTE THE AUTHOR'S INTENT

Think about five basic text structures (description, sequence, problem/solution, cause/effect, compare/contrast) and how they are used by writers to organize and present their ideas and information in both fiction and nonfiction. When writing fiction, these structures can be used to move a story forward. For example, let's say a character is trying to make a decision about which of two items to purchase. In this situation, the writer may choose to have the character think through a compare/contrast scenario where the character thinks, "I could wear either pair to school, but if I choose these I could also wear them to the party on Friday…." Another option would be to consider a cause/effect scenario where the character thinks, "If I buy this one, all my money will be gone and then I couldn't go to…." When writing nonfiction, these text structures may be more obvious as the writer employs a structure to help the reader gain greater insight and understanding. For example, if writing about human-caused threats to sea life, the writer may use description to present the problem, offer a cause/effect connection to show the impact, then use compare/contrast to show the difference between a threatened species and one that isn't. (You can find a printable graphic organizer for the Five Basic Text Structures That Help Move a Story Forward at scholastic.com/URAResources.)

In each visit, you will notice more and more. But this process is not a treasure hunt—you are not taking a stack of books and a ledger sheet and keeping a tally of which book(s) offer the most connections to curriculum or standards. We do not develop strong, lasting bonds of friendship by going to social functions in search of people who can serve our purposes in life. Rather, we live our lives and people cross our paths. We find some of them engaging, intriguing, and fascinating. We come to know them over time. We develop a true friendship and build trust and caring.

A Best Friend Book has sufficient substance and depth to hold up to many visits across the year. A good BFB creates a solid foundation for other work in the classroom community or curriculum. These books are selected because each time you return to a Best Friend Book, you may find yet another point of entry and leave with new or deeper insight. While there are numerous books with tremendous potential for extension or engagement, a Best Friend Book is one that invites self-reflection and can be revisited to explore language, life, text structures, text features, the craft of writing, and/or content-area insights.

Ultimately, we want Best Friend Books to live in the minds and hearts of each reader-writer in the classroom. We want students to be able to call upon these titles when they are navigating their way through another text as a reader or when constructing a text as a writer. When conferring with a student (or when students are conferring with a peer), these Best Friend Books are also present and waiting to join in the conversation and offer insight.

A Best Friend Book is one that can transform our reading and writing as we revisit it multiple times across the year. Each visit offers a new reason to think about the book and gives students a new understanding of the potential of literature. The familiarity they'll develop will build insights that will become touchstones for your conferring work in reading and writing workshops.

Throughout this book, we will look at the ways in which we can use Best Friend Books with our children to get the most out of the read-aloud experience and create deep connections.

WHAT THE RESEARCH SAYS

Every time we enter a text as a reader, we receive a writing lesson: how to spell, punctuate, use proper grammar, structure a sentence or paragraph, and organize a text. We also learn the many purposes writing serves and the different genres and formats it assumes to serve these varied purposes. (Duke, 2014; Krashen, 2004; Kittle, in press; Laminack & Wadsworth, 2015)

Spotlight on Lester Videos

In my work in schools, staff-development workshops, and conferences around the country, I focus on the art and function of reading aloud. I am frequently asked if I have made any videos that illustrate the techniques and joys of the read-aloud. Throughout this book, you will see places where you can stop and review a video demonstration of my work with several different read-alouds as well as more information about using Best Friend Books. Look for the "Spotlight on Lester Video" icon as you read. In each of these videos, I think aloud to let you see what I consider as I make decisions about my read-aloud instruction. My hope is that *The Ultimate Read-Aloud Resource* will provide you with new options, new energy, and a new commitment to the art of the read-aloud and to the tremendous potential that it holds for your students.

**SPOTLIGHT ON
LESTER VIDEO**

BFB Home Visits

Best friends often come home with you for a visit. When they do, you introduce them to your family, explore the things you have in common, and learn even more about each other. Now imagine bringing a Best Friend Book along for a home visit. Because these books are familiar to everyone in the classroom community, every student will have specific insights about each title. The characters in fiction and the information in nonfiction will have been the topic of many discussions and may have filtered into the conversations at home already. Let parents/caregivers know that you are introducing a small set of books to the class as Best Friend Books. Explain what that means and how this is different from your typical read-aloud books. You'll find a sample letter to parents in the BFB Home Visit section on scholastic.com/URAResources. You'll also find materials to help students introduce these books to their families and then read them together. The goal here is to bring a familiar character or topic home for a visit to extend the conversations, insights, and connections. The conversations from school will most certainly spill over into the talk at home, and the conversations from home hold the potential to bring new dimensions to the conversations at school. Check out all of the materials and videos related to BFB Home Visits by looking for the icon throughout the book.

HOME VISIT
scholastic.com/URAResources

Who Should Read This Book?

As I wrote this book, I thought of all the adults who work with children and have the opportunity to read aloud to them. I thought of the children whose faces grow intense with engagement when the tension rises in a good story and whose smiles break open into a thousand bits of laughter in the funny parts. I thought of the children who lose themselves in the new information and take delight in discovering new words. I wrote as if I were talking to the educators I work with around the country almost every week of the year. When I provide staff development or speak at a conference, I am always aware that among the folks sitting in the audience there will be classroom teachers, Title I teachers, literacy coaches, staff developers, librarians/media specialists, principals, and other administrators—I wrote for them. I wrote knowing that every decision we make must be measured by the answer to one question—"Will this be good for children?" I hope as you read you will be able to say "YES!" when you are thinking about whether you should make read-aloud an essential, nonnegotiable part of every single day for every single child.

Teachers

Clearly, you are the front line in the work of leading children to fall in love with language and literature and all sorts of nonfiction texts as they become readers and writers. You are the ones who select the books, who set the tone of the experience, who lure children into a web of texts of all kinds. As teachers, you are the daily dose of read-aloud. Your voices are the ones that linger in the minds of children as they romp around on the playground, stand in line for lunch, or load onto the bus and head for home at the end of the day. You are the ones who introduce new topics and revisit favorite authors and illustrators or bring in new ones. You are the ones who deepen children's understanding of genre and open the doors to new ways of looking at life and the world around us.

Teachers, as I wrote, I envisioned you surrounded by students, captivating them with nothing more than a Best Friend Book and your voice. *The Ultimate Read-Aloud Resource* is designed to deepen your understanding of the power, purpose, and art of the read-aloud experience in your classroom. The text will offer three intentions for read-aloud—to inspire, to invest, and to instruct—and give you specific suggestions for living out those intentions with each read-aloud experience. In addition, there are specific connections to learning theory and to language/literacy development.

Librarians and Media Specialists

Oh, you lucky people! You get to be with all the books and all the kids. What could be better? *The Ultimate Read-Aloud Resource* offers you a means for promoting read-aloud experiences throughout the school day. The three intentions provide a framework for helping your colleagues organize and present books across the curriculum in careful, thoughtful, and purposeful ways. That gives you one more way to assist teachers in the never-ending effort to connect children and books. The accompanying videos will heighten your attention to the design of a book and the signals the book contains to guide your use of tone, intensity, pacing, and mood when you read aloud in the library or in a classroom.

Literacy Coaches and Staff Developers

In your role, you have the opportunity to promote read-aloud experiences as essential instructional intentions. But as you know, talking about it, giving all the reasons for doing more, and even providing the books don't always make it the most effective experience. *The Ultimate Read-Aloud Resource* explains how to gather a study group in a close examination of the art of reading aloud. The text and videos will assist you in coaching your colleagues through the selection of Best Friend Books, articulating the intention for each read-aloud experience, and attending to the specific signals in the text. You'll have the opportunity to move through old favorites and new titles with new insights, bringing the life of the text to the surface through attention to tone, intensity, pacing, and mood.

Principals and Other Administrators

The Ultimate Read-Aloud Resource can deepen your insights into the values of read-aloud at a time when there is greater attention to accountability. Use this tool to justify time spent reading aloud to children in the classrooms of your building. Use this tool to recognize the qualities of an artful, intentional, and meaningful read-aloud.

Why Read-Aloud Matters

"Reading aloud with children is known to be the single most important activity for building the knowledge and skills they will eventually require for learning to read."

—MARILYN JAGER ADAMS, READING RESEARCHER

Perhaps the first hurdle in the teaching of reading is to build the love of books and stories and information. We live in a world of instant access—all we have to do is tap a screen or speak a question into our phones and an answer will follow. Not so long ago, I was working in San Antonio, Texas, and had an afternoon free. As I was strolling along the Riverwalk, I passed a young couple with two small children. The infant was tucked in a sling one parent wore like a kangaroo pouch, and the toddler was buckled into a stroller being pushed by the other parent. What struck me about this little family was that the parents were chatting away, the infant appeared to be sleeping, and the toddler was busily engaged with an iPad. The four of them were strolling amidst an array of birds and insects and trees and flowers and music and aromas and boats and water and food and laughter and people. The toddler never looked up. She didn't point to anything and ask about it. The parents didn't stop and kneel down next to her to point out and name all the interesting things that could have broadened the child's repertoire of sights and sounds and smells and words. Oh, the words they could have used. I ached over the missed opportunities to connect the real world to vocabulary.

A little further down the path, I took a seat at a small table on the sidewalk and ordered a drink and a bite to eat. I watched people with children and wondered what stories they would tell next week when they went back to their regular lives, when the Riverwalk was just a memory. I wondered what bits of their trip would filter into their talk, and what new language and concepts would be lifted to connect with books they may read. I sat there and I wondered.

I hear the demands to raise scores in our schools. I see the impact of the pressure to get more done in less time to meet standards. And I wonder. I wonder what we lose when we let go of those small moments when we kneel down next to a child and look at the world from their level. Where is the fascination with a ladybug strolling across a leaf or an inchworm arcing and stretching its way up a stem? Where are those moments when a child giggles with excitement at the flutter of wings and the sudden flight of a bird? Will we lose the intense natural interest children bring to the worlds of their imagination? Those experiences, it seems to me, are the building blocks of story. The shared experiences, the new discoveries, the fresh new words that tickle a little one's tongue; those are the building blocks of story. In our rush to raise scores, to cover more in less time, we cannot lose sight of the notion that we are raising humans, young and impressionable humans. With that said, let's remind ourselves of the need for play and exploration. Let's remind ourselves of the power of pretend and imagination.

Let's remind ourselves that story is a way we recall experience and construct meaning and negotiate our ideas and open a world of new possibilities. The curriculum we once crafted for our first graders, we now deliver to kindergarten children. What's more, in some schools, we ask children as young as six to choose the college they plan to attend once they graduate from high school. This seems a tall order for young children who often don't fully understand what college is (Pappano, 2015). Why all the rush to move children into adulthood? I wonder.

SPOTLIGHT ON LESTER VIDEO

Lester Answers Some Common Questions About Read-Alouds

scholastic.com/URAResources

How I Was Introduced to the Read-Aloud

What comes to mind when you hear someone talking about the read-aloud? Do you flash back to your own school days and see yourself settling into your desk right after lunch? Is your head resting on your folded arms? Do you hear your teacher's voice recounting the last few events of the pages read aloud yesterday? Maybe your mind takes you to the library, that palace of books where the librarian gathered you and others near enough to get swept away in the current of language flowing on the human voice. Perhaps it isn't a school memory at all. Perhaps you are taken back even further, back to your earliest childhood memories. Does talk of read-aloud evoke the smell of your mother, the tender voice of your grandmother, or the secure feeling of snuggling in close to your father? Is it a particular story or poem you recall, or is it the sound of a voice? Is it the words of the story or the cadence and the rhythm of the language? Is it the reading or the undivided attention showered upon you in those magical moments? What is it about read-aloud experiences that can leave such lasting and powerful memories long after the book is closed… long after…?

Lester, in third grade, beginning his lifelong love of books and the read-aloud

My earliest memories of read-aloud take me back to an apartment over the garage behind my Grandmother Thompson's house in Heflin, Alabama. I was four years old. My brother Scott was six, already in school and already reading. I remember these little boxes that came in the mail from time to time. Each box held two books, and those became instant favorites. Each night I took my perch on the wide arm of an overstuffed chair. My brother sat nestled in the seat next to Mother with the book spread across their laps. His slender fingers trailed across the page as that music—released from his mouth—lingered in the air. I basked in the glory of the rhythm, I lusted after that magic, and I coveted the nest where complete adoration flowed from mother to son. I was addicted to the whole idea of it. Of course there were others who read aloud to me. But none had the same impact in my most formative years.

But the most lasting impression of read-aloud was etched into my memory in the library of Cleburne County Elementary School in Heflin, Alabama. The year was 1964. I was eight years old, and our third-grade class made weekly visits to the library on Thursdays. I looked forward to those visits with unwrapping-a-birthday-present eagerness. I longed for Thursday, though not primarily for the opportunity to roam around the stacks of old books standing at attention, spine-to-spine with new ones. I longed for Thursday for the gift of Mrs. Hand's voice, that slow, deliberate, carefully delivered voice of books. Mrs. Hand had a distinctive voice. Low and resonant like a cello. Smooth and lush like expensive velvet. Slow and unhurried like pouring honey on a February morning. It was as if Mrs. Hand loved one thing more than sharing all those books, only one thing. Us.

"As we share the words and pictures, the ideas and viewpoints, the rhythms and rhymes, the pain and comfort, and the hopes and fears and big issues of life that we encounter together in the pages of a book, we connect through minds and hearts with our children and bond closely in a secret society associated with the books we have shared. The fire of literacy is created by the emotional sparks between a child, a book, and the person reading."

—MEM FOX

When she read, it was clear that she was sharing a treasure, and that this was a most special once-a-week treasure that she held just for us. She had such control over the elements of an artful read-aloud—tone, intensity, pace, and mood. Looking back, I am convinced that my own fascination with the sounds of books read aloud—the very music of the written word played on the instrument of a well-tuned human voice—is grounded in the third-grade memories of our school librarian, Mrs. Hand, sharing her love of books, words, and us in half-hour installments once each week.

"The unique language of books and literacy is learned the way any language is learned—by using and living it as a way of life."

—**JOHN SHEFELBINE**

Mrs. Hand was charged with such important duties as teaching us to use the card catalog, leading us to pledge our allegiance to the Dewey decimal system, and helping us to become adept at locating the books we needed. Although she was the undisputed queen of that palace of books, she had a deep and abiding love for reading and, more important for us, for the children of our tiny community tucked away in rural Alabama. It was that love that guided her in the application of her knowledge. She was a wise woman, and she understood something essential about becoming literate, something so obvious, yet so rare in the daily practice of our schools. Mrs. Hand understood that mastering the Dewey decimal system, becoming an ace navigator of the card catalog, and developing the ability to locate any title in less than 60 seconds would be useless skills unless we first fell in love with books. She understood that *function* precedes *form*, that the *need to know* drives learning *how to do*, that *passion* for anything is a most powerful driving force in the life of any human being.

Mrs. Hand was not wasting time reading *The Boxcar Children* aloud to our class. She didn't read those weekly installments because she had nothing else planned or because she had planned too little to fill up the time and keep us focused. She didn't read to us because she was too lazy to get off the stool. She didn't read to us because she was too unprofessional to teach us those important tools and skills of library life. She read aloud to us to woo us in, to seduce our minds and souls into the spell of reading. Like the call of the sirens from ancient Greece, she read to us artfully and with great intention. Mrs. Hand knew what she was doing. She *read aloud* to us deliberately. She selected books specifically for us, books she *knew we'd fall in love with*. She knew that once Henry and Jesse and Violet and precious little Benny found that old, abandoned boxcar, we'd be utterly and hopelessly in love. And she was right. As she read, I pictured myself romping through the pine thickets around our house and stumbling upon a boxcar. I so longed to be Henry, that brave and strong big brother who took charge and made sure all his siblings were cared for. But the truth is that I more closely identified with Benny. I was the younger brother, the weaker one, the sweet and naïve one. And when Benny found that cherished pink cup with the chip in the rim, the one his sisters scoured with a bit of soap and sand, I could taste the cold milk he drank from it. I could feel the chip as the rim touched my lips. And that was my first experience with becoming lost inside a book, falling in with and *living* alongside the characters. I was *forever changed* as a reader. And today, I am convinced it was in that moment that *I was born as a writer*.

WHAT THE RESEARCH SAYS

Reading has cognitive consequences that extend beyond its immediate task of creating meaning from a particular passage. Furthermore, these consequences are reciprocal and exponential in nature. Accumulated over time—spiraling either upward or downward—they carry profound implications for the development of a wide range of cognitive capabilities. (Cunningham & Zibulsky, 2014; Duke et al., 2011; Stephens, Harste, & Clyde, 2019)

The Seven Functions of Language

Michael Halliday (1973) identified the following seven functions of language that may help fine-tune our thinking about making our read-aloud experiences intentional. Language serves multiple purposes; indeed, because language is functional, it's relatively easy for young children to learn their mother tongue. They quickly learn that they can get their needs met and interact with others in fulfilling ways by using language. Keeping these language functions in mind as you share books with your students may extend the learning possibilities:

INSTRUMENTAL Language for getting things done, for satisfying one's needs

REGULATORY Language for controlling the behavior of others

INTERACTIONAL Language for maintaining and establishing relationships

PERSONAL Language for expressing personality and individuality

HEURISTIC Language for finding things out, for exploring the environment

IMAGINATIVE Language as a means of creating a world of one's own

REPRESENTATIONAL Language for conveying information

Let's take a moment to examine each of these functions as they may relate to our intentions for reading aloud to inspire our students as readers and writers. You can find a printable graphic organizer for The Seven Functions of Language at scholastic.com/URAResources.

Instrumental Language

The language for getting things done—instrumental—can be heard in numerous read-aloud experiences. We are witnesses to the use of instrumental language when a writer uses language that enables a character to accomplish his or her desires and needs. If we select books thoughtfully, our students will hear the way characters use language to meet their needs, accomplish their goals, and make their wishes known each time we read aloud. As a result, we broaden our students' understanding of the potentials of both spoken and written language. Consider Max in *Bunny Cakes* (Wells, 1997). He needed "red-hot marshmallow squirters" for his earthworm cake, so he added that to the list Ruby gave him to take to the grocer. Max knows the power of language to get things done, even though he is learning to control written language. We see another example in the comments from the hens in *Three Hens and a Peacock* (Laminack, 2011) when they are planning what to wear for their day by the road stopping cars.

Regulatory Language

By attempting to control the behavior of others—evident in the notes and signs and warnings sprinkled throughout a book—we are using regulatory language. These may be sent by one character to another or encountered by a character in the plot of a story. Regulatory language may be sprinkled into the art as signs or labels or captions. Examples of regulatory language may also be seen in the speech of one character giving direction to another, as in *Saturdays and Teacakes* (Laminack, 2004): "My mother always said, '*You stop and look both ways when you get to Chandler's. I don't care if the light is green. I'll hear about it if you don't.*'" We can also call attention to the use of regulatory language in situations where one character is trying to be in control. Consider *The Recess Queen* (O'Neill, 2002), when Mean Jean says, "'Say WHAT?' Mean Jean growled. 'Say WHO?' Mean Jean howled. 'Say YOU! Just who do you think you're talking to?'" In nonfiction we may see warnings and cautions attempting to guide the reader's actions. These may be included in procedures, experiments, etc. These examples demonstrate for our students that language can be used to control the behavior of others.

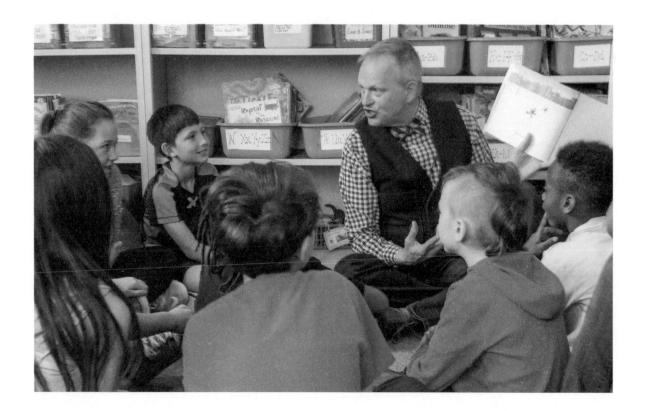

Interactional Language

Interactional language is used to maintain and establish relationships. We can demonstrate the function of interactional language through a read-aloud of *A Letter to Amy* (Keats, 1998). Peter's letter to Amy extending an invitation to his birthday party is a clear example of written language intended to maintain a friendship. Other examples can be found in the delightful books of Alma Flor Ada, *Dear Peter Rabbit* (2006), *Yours Truly, Goldilocks* (2001), and *With Love, Little Red Hen* (2004), in which letters are sent between the characters of our favorite stories from childhood. In addition, you may find it helpful to point out incidences in other favorite read-alouds where characters are using dialogue to begin or continue friendships. Each of these will be yet another demonstration of the many ways we use both oral and written language.

Personal Language

Personal language—used to express personality or individuality—can be found in most any read-aloud in which the writer reveals a character through playful word choice. Junie B. Jones, the spirited young character featured by Barbara Parks in numerous books, comes to mind as a good example of a character whose language is part of her personality. You will find similar examples in the Amelia Bedelia books created by Peggy Parish. For other examples of personal language, share Helen Lester's *Hooway for Wodney Wat*, or Roald Dahl's *The BFG*, or Judy Blume's books featuring the effervescent younger brother, Fudge. In each case, the writer's choice of language for these characters etches a lasting memory in the mind of the reader and listener.

Personality and voice can be found in nonfiction as well. Consider the playful language in *Burp!* by Diane Swanson (2001): "Never mind where you are, who you're

WHAT THE RESEARCH SAYS

"One of the most important and challenging tasks that young children encounter when they begin their formal schooling is listening to directions, and children who can make sense of the requests or directives they receive are likely to fare better than students who need more time to decipher a sentence and determine the meaning of an unfamiliar word." (Cunningham, A., & Zibulsky, J., 2014, pp. 21–22) with or what's going on in your life, sometimes you're just plain hungry. Your body has absorbed the last of the nutrients you gave it, you're running out of energy, and YOU WANT FOOD."

Heuristic Language

Heuristic language, used for finding things out or for exploring the environment, is quite common in classrooms. Heuristic language can be heard in the hundreds of questions asked each day in a typical classroom. We can also see it in the all-about and how-to books and the information books in our nonfiction collections. We can feature this use of language through read-aloud experiences with selections from Gail Gibbons, Melissa Stewart, Cathryn Sill, Seymour Simon, Diane Siebert, Nicola Davies, and Thomas Locker. Many of our favorite nonfiction writers will give us ample opportunity to use language to find out and explore.

"No wonder experts tell us that children need to hear a thousand stories read aloud before they begin to learn to read for themselves. A thousand! That sounds daunting. But when we do the sums, it isn't as bad as we might think. Three stories a day will deliver us a thousand stories in one year alone, let alone in the four or five years prior to school."

—MEM FOX

WHAT THE RESEARCH SAYS

It's not surprising to learn that there is a correlation between a child developing oral language skills and the sophistication of the questions she's asked during the read-aloud. Researchers kept track of what parents said to their 27-month-olds while reading aloud to them; sure enough, open-ended questions and sophisticated prompts that sparked further exploration of the book seemed to promote expressive language skills and a more robust vocabulary— evident when these same children were tested again between the ages of 30 and 42 months. Open-ended questions and sophisticated prompts (beyond "yes or no" questions and simple directives such as "turn the page" and "point to the picture") encourage deep reading, deep discussion, deep thinking—and deep learning! (Cunningham & Zibulsky, 2014; Sharer, 2018)

Imaginative Language

The language of the imagination is used to create a world of one's own. Young children seem quite comfortable with pretending and talking about things and situations as if they were real. They create towns with blocks, go grocery shopping in the dramatic play areas of their classrooms, and travel to the moon just by climbing up a ladder. Each time we read aloud a book in which the author takes us on a journey of suspended logic—where we imagine and pretend—we are wallowing in imaginative language. So when the children in *Roxaboxen* (McLerran, 2004) create a town using rocks to outline the buildings, and create their own rules and government and currency, they use imaginative language. They talk about imaginary things as if they were real. Through books such as this, we help our students see imaginative language at work. Clearly then, any work of fantasy, folktale, or fairy tale capable of evoking the imagination can be read aloud, showing yet another function for both written and oral language.

WHAT THE RESEARCH SAYS

The research shows that reading fiction has a profound impact on language and literacy development, including vocabulary, spelling, and grammar. In a recent study, frequency of voluntary reading of both "middle-brow" and "high-brow" fiction was a very strong predictor of vocabulary size. All this makes reading demanding nonfiction texts possible.

Studies also show that fiction exposes readers to other views of the world and other ways of thinking, and increases the ability to deal with uncertainty, which is crucial for problem-solving. "Fiction is the bridge between everyday conversational language and academic language and increases empathy and the ability to deal with uncertainty." (Krashen, 2015. See also: Beers & Probst, 2017; and Djikic et al., 2013)

Imagination is an essential factor in invention and creative projects. Consider biographies that reveal how an individual imagined possibilities and spoke and wrote about them in the process of bringing them into reality. Help your students to recognize how imaginative language also contributes to reality.

Representational Language

For a striking example of representational language, take a look at *The Handmade Alphabet* by Laura Rankin, in which sign language is demonstrated in beautiful language and art. The National Council of Teachers of English's Orbis Pictus Awards are a good source of outstanding books that convey facts and information. (See www.ncte.org/elem/awards/orbispictus.)

"*This year, we are going to read many different books, but there will be some books that we like so much that we are going to come back to them over and over again and discuss them at length, because they have big ideas in them that we don't want to stop talking about. . . . When books become really important to us in this way, we'll come back to them again and again.*"

—TASHA TOPP LAMAN & ANNE GARDNER ALEXANDER

Closing Thoughts

There is no doubt that read-aloud matters. The research is clear, but more important, any adult can bear witness to the power of reading aloud to children. Imagine how that power intensifies when we select a small set of stories that we read again and again. Through repeated visits with a single story, children deepen insights about how language works. Together we discover how writers reveal characters. We uncover the relationships between characters and setting. We explore the impact of setting upon plot. We gain insight into the potentials for secondary characters in the development of the story. We begin to understand how tension is built, and come to recognize the markers of a story arc. Through repeated visits with nonfiction we begin to understand how writers organize information. We broaden and deepen our vocabulary through exposure to topic-specific terms paired with examples in language and illustration. We come to understand the functions and potential uses of text features. And we develop greater insight into the vast array of information waiting on the pages of nonfiction. We visit this collection of carefully selected books again and again because conceptual development takes time. As we visit and revisit a Best Friend Book, we come back to the book with more language, more insight, better questions, and deeper connections. And once we grasp these essential literary concepts, we can begin to move out to broader experiences and apply those insights in new situations.

Toward the Intentional Read-Aloud

"After nearly three decades of gathering first graders around me to read a story, I believe that a wealth of experiences plus a love of reading are the keys to a happy life."

—MARIA WALTHER, FIRST-GRADE TEACHER AND AUTHOR

There was a time when read-aloud was as firmly entrenched in the daily routine of school as going to lunch. Teachers read aloud to their students with the regularity of school bells announcing the beginning of a new day. No one questioned the practice—what could possibly be wrong with something so sensible, so enjoyable, something so thoroughly satisfying as reading aloud to students? Who would dare question the motives of a teacher sitting at the front of a room on a tall stool, holding an open book, while captivating the full attention of an entire classroom of children? And think of it—all this with nothing more than the human voice and well-crafted language.

Yet as I work in schools around the country, teachers report feeling they don't have time for read-aloud in their increasingly busy days. They report feeling they can hardly justify time spent reading to children, and that to do so makes them feel subversive. How very sad that something so pure, something so very simple, has become suspect. How very sad that we have reached a point in schooling where as teachers we feel we must justify our every decision, even the most basic, commonsensical decisions about taking time to read aloud to children. So I invite you to join me in an effort to reclaim read-aloud for our students and, yes, even for ourselves. Let's reinvent this tried-and-true practice, this commonsensical standard in the education of our children. Let's reclaim this sensible source of endless *inspiration*. Let's reinvigorate this trusted means of *investing* in the minds of our students and opening their lives to a world beyond their own imaginations. Let's reenvision read-aloud as a respected means of instruction. Let's make every read-aloud *intentional*. Toward that goal, we must be thoughtful in our selection of texts to read aloud. We must be clear in our own minds about *why* we are reading a particular title. I am advocating for reading aloud with the frequency of birdsong and with the zeal of a street performer. I am advocating for reading aloud from a wide array of titles that represent a variety of authors and illustrators and genres and topics. I am advocating for reading aloud several times each day. But I am also advocating that each classroom have a small collection, ideally five fiction and five nonfiction titles—Best Friend Books—that are read aloud again and again to build the level of familiarity that one would have with a best friend.

SPOTLIGHT ON LESTER VIDEO

What Makes a Read-Aloud Intentional?

scholastic.com/URAResources

GENERAL READ-ALOUD EXPERIENCES:

- Serve as a foundation of a solid, thoughtful language and literacy program

- Create scaffolds for connecting understanding to independent reading and writing

- Support content in every subject area by building background knowledge that supports inquiry

- Nourish the intellect (listening comprehension is built through daily experiences hearing texts read aloud, participating in discussions of those texts, and making connections with those texts)

- Demonstrate thinking as we and our students share personal connections, make connections to other texts, take in new information, and adjust personal views

- Provide opportunities for deeper reflection that may lead to repeated reading of the same text

- Develop and refine topic-specific vocabulary essential to content-area learning

- Provide exposure to text structures, helping our students understand how texts can be organized and noting why specific structures are used

- Provide exposure to a variety of text types and help our students recognize the differences between nonfiction and fiction, poetry and prose

- Provide a demonstration of phrased, fluent reading, showing the function of tone, intensity, pacing, and mood

- Create a literary community in the classroom where a pool of shared meanings and a common language can develop

- Expand children's literary knowledge by developing their understanding of plot, character, themes, and setting

- Build a repertoire of genres, favorite authors, and favorite illustrators

- Expand our students' notions of writer's craft and how craft helps the reader construct meaning across genres and text types

BEST FRIEND BOOK READ-ALOUD EXPERIENCES:

- Build a collection of texts that all students in the classroom community know intimately

- Bring a set of characters into the classroom community that students know the way they know a best friend

- Bring a set of topics into the classroom community that students share interest in and develop a common vocabulary around

- Establish a deeper understanding of the format and function of text features commonly found in nonfiction

- Result in a small collection of books that all students carry in their hearts and in their heads

- Establish a literary knowledge base common to all members of the classroom community

- Establish intimate familiarity with each Best Friend author's writing craft and unique techniques for creating clarity and interest to engage readers

- Showcase the lovely language—such as surprising turns of phrase, playful and poetic prose, and musical phrasing—unique to each Best Friend author

- Heighten awareness of the ways in which print and graphics work together to enhance meaning and enjoyment

- Invite an "insider's understanding" of the ways in which literature illuminates, expands, and enhances life

- Help establish an emotional connection with particular authors, themes, topics, and genres—and reading!

To make read-aloud *intentional,* I believe that we must be as thoughtful in our planning as we are when selecting manipulatives for mathematics or when establishing the flow of a classroom. We must select the books we will read with the same care we take in designing centers or in setting up a science lab. We must be as diligent in considering our reasons for reading aloud as we are in selecting the focus of a mini-lesson in reading and writing workshops. In short, we must pay careful attention to our *intentions* for the read-aloud.

QUESTIONS TO ASK YOURSELF:

- Why do I read aloud to my students?

- What are my expectations for the experience?

- What result or product do I hope for?

- How will my students be different for living through these experiences with me?

- Am I hoping to motivate them to explore a topic or genre?

- Am I inviting them to meet a new author or illustrator?

- Am I leading them to compare the organizational framework of this text with a favorite known by all?

- Am I simply reading today for some future benefit, investing the time now to connect future instruction later?

- Am I reading to introduce specific vocabulary that will be essential in understanding the concepts for a unit of study in a subject area?

- Am I reading to contrast the multiple meanings of troublesome words?

- Am I reading to raise awareness of a targeted issue?

- Am I reading to model a specific reading strategy or skill?

- Am I reading to draw them in, to lure them into wanting to read more for themselves?

- Am I reading to bank images and language we will draw upon in an upcoming study?

As I see it, all these *intentions* can be easily grouped under three broad reasons for reading aloud. We make read-aloud intentional when we purposely select texts and times with the intent to *inspire*, *invest*, or *instruct*. (Allyn & Morrell, 2016; Harvey & Ward, 2017; Miller & Sharp, 2018; Scharer, 2018; and Stephens et al., 2019)

Reading Aloud to Inspire

Mrs. Hand read to my third-grade class with no other obvious intention than to captivate our hearts. She was reading to *inspire* new devotees. She wanted us to love reading, to lust after language, to crave time with books. Mrs. Hand knew we had to fall in love before we would ever see the need for strategies and skills that would give us the stamina to live through a chapter book or more dense information book independently. Remember, Mrs. Hand understood some essentials about learning. Let me quickly remind you—she understood that *function* precedes *form*, that the *need to know* drives learning *how to do*, that *passion* for anything is a most powerful driving force in the life of any human being. In other words, if we teach them *how* without teaching them *why*, we leave them in a situation where they don't know *when*. Knowing how to do something without knowing why you do it leaves you at a loss about *when* that new learning is needed.

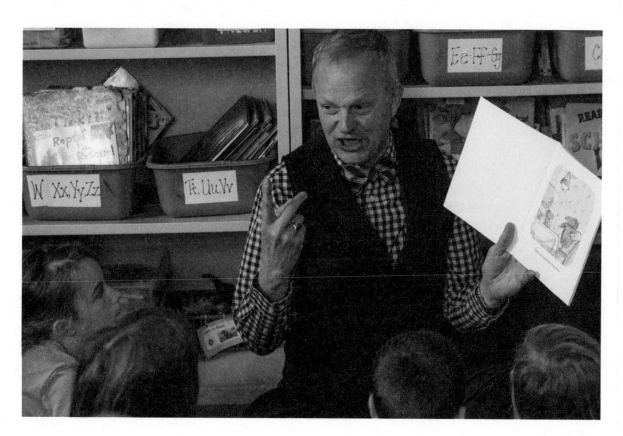

Think about the teenagers you have known. One very common passion driving them, virtually *all* of them, is the vision of driving a vehicle. How is it that young people can become so enamored with the ability to drive? What plants the seed of the notion that driving is something desirable? We live in a very mobile society in which people equate mobility with freedom. From the time children are born, they are on the go. Children are strapped into car seats several times each week as the caregivers run errands, drive them to and from babysitters, day care, school, after-school events, and more. Children see the ability to drive demonstrated over and over without explicit intentions for making them good drivers. Rather, it is the mobility, the ability to accomplish so many things independently without reliance on someone else, that is the lure. I have met very few teenagers who were not absolutely *lusting* after a driver's license by the time they were 14 years old. And remember: All they have is the consistent demonstration of the *function* of this ability. Their experience with drivers is an ever-present demonstration of all the freedom this *skill* and *ability* brings with it. It takes no cajoling, no bribes, no points or pizzas. It takes little more than being witness in daily life to the *function* of the act itself.

So what can we do to create that same lusting after language, books, reading? Perhaps it is as simple as driving. We demonstrate by our daily actions the essential *functions* of reading in the life of a human being. The point here is that read-aloud experiences can be thoughtfully planned to demonstrate the functions of language to inspire our students to read and write. So each time we read aloud, we demonstrate that language has purpose and power. We demonstrate that as readers and writers we strengthen our ability to use language each time we read or listen to someone else read. We put that growing strength to use each time we write and speak. As teachers, we have both the insight and the knowledge to select books carefully, thoughtfully, and purposefully. As teachers, we can decide what to feature or draw attention to as we read aloud. As teachers, we can lead our students to understand and appreciate the potentials of language that can inspire them to be readers and writers themselves. One way we

WHAT THE RESEARCH SAYS

Researchers suggest that the most valuable aspect of the read-aloud activity is that it gives children experience with decontextualized language, requiring them to make sense of ideas that are about something beyond the here and now. (Beck & Sandora, 2016; Beck & McKeown, 2001; Scharer, 2018)

do that is by being keenly aware of the functions or purposes that language serves in our lives and making those more visible for our students. And when we revisit a Best Friend Book again and again, we have the time to slow down, to look closely at a single element and notice how writers lay the groundwork for our work as readers.

Reading Aloud to Develop Language and Concepts

When we *invest* in anything, we expect to make small installments over long periods of time with the understanding that dividends will not be collected until much later. Talk with anyone nearing retirement and they will tell you how very important it is to make contributions of any size as often as possible to the general fund. Retirement age is too late to begin thinking about what we *could* have done or *might* have done or *should* have done to live well in our later years.

Likewise, if *investment* is the specific intention of a read-aloud, then we select books for the potential each of them holds. We think in advance of the outcome or product we desire. So with that in mind, we begin with a close look at the specific subject and the unit of study. We identify the core understanding needed for successful completion and select books that will enable us to create scaffolds through exposure to images, specific vocabulary, and concepts that new learning can be built upon. We sequence these texts both in a way that will be logical for the learners and will scaffold the concepts in the study.

"Reading aloud is not a cure-all. Not quite. But it is such a wonderful antidote for turning on turned-off readers and brightening up dull writing that I feel it's worthwhile to plead again for its regular occurrence in every classroom, not only those classrooms at the younger end of school. . . . The value of my writing increases before my very eye, beneath my very pen. The investment in listening, I have found, pays dividends."

—MEM FOX

Then, in careful, thoughtfully planned, and patient installments, we layer each read-aloud to establish a collective common ground of the classroom community, and we pace the presentation of texts to the ability of our students to process the essential information. The main point here is to *invest* the time *now* to read aloud from these specifically selected texts with the expressed intention that the time spent now will yield significant dividends during the actual study as it unfolds. Think of it this way: Time spent reading aloud on this end helps to establish the common ground that you connect with comfortably as you begin the more in-depth work of the unit of study. For a detailed listing of books carefully selected to support read-alouds intended to invest time, language, and concepts, see *Learning Under the Influence of Language and Literature* (Laminack and Wadsworth, 2006), *Reading Aloud Across the Curriculum* (Laminack & Wadsworth, 2006), and *The Ramped-Up Read Aloud: What to Notice as You Turn the Page* (Walther, 2019).

Reading Aloud to Instruct

When we set out to instruct another person, there is typically a relationship established that defines our role. The instructor is assumed to be competent, masterful, accomplished, and perhaps even artful in something that the apprentice or student *needs* or *wants* to learn. But as teachers, our work is done in an institution of learning where student attendance is mandatory. Our students are not seeking us out because of our passion and competence, or because of our accomplishments or our artful application of knowledge and skill. Our students aren't even selecting to be in our specific classrooms. Their choices are limited from the start. It isn't their drive to know, their passion for a topic, that sends them out on a mission to find a mentor. So we can't assume that all of our students are eager to learn what we have been charged to teach.

Let's explore how a read-aloud intended to instruct can be a most beneficial experience in this situation. Assume for a moment that your students are expected to study story elements in language arts. Let's further assume that the curriculum expects your students to be able to compare and contrast two different ways a writer uses dialogue.

One way this might be approached is through traditional lessons from language arts textbooks, follow-up exercises, and a homework assignment. Clearly, most teachers are adept at extending these more traditional approaches with interesting options that make the work more engaging. However, vocabulary and background knowledge may be uneven. Some may read the textbook and gather information they simply transfer to a worksheet or exercise, while others see the examples and are able to apply the information to classroom lessons almost immediately. It would be quite possible, then, for students in both these situations to "do well" on the assignment without developing any deeper understanding of how to transfer the information into their own writing work.

SPOTLIGHT ON LESTER VIDEO

What Makes a Read-Aloud Instructional?

scholastic.com/URAResources

If we follow Frank Smith's idea that children are built to learn from the company they keep (2004), then what does that suggest for us about reading aloud with intentions to instruct? Can we actually read aloud as instruction? Yes, we can.

The key, as I see it, lies in our intentions. If we intend to instruct through the read-aloud experience, then much rests on the sense of community we have established and on the very careful selection of books. As with any intentional instruction, we must know what we expect our students to learn as a result of the experience. We begin with those expectations, and we place them alongside our knowledge of our students. We assess their existing background knowledge, including their current insights and misunderstandings. Through initial conversations, we determine their facility with vocabulary related to the topic and their ability to speak with specificity using that vocabulary. These insights aid us in selecting books to read aloud and also serve as common ground for developing and extending communal concepts about this topic.

So, with the example of comparing and contrasting dialogue, we would select two titles from our Best Friend Books where the authors use dialogue for different purposes. For example, dialogue in one book may be used to give us insight into the character's thoughts. In another book, it is to give the main character a scaffold to reveal the tension in the plot. Revisiting two familiar books puts us in a position where we can turn to a specific scene and point out explicitly how dialogue is being used.

Closing Thoughts

Reading aloud can be a powerful tool in our instruction. The right books in the hands of a skillful teacher can be focused to inspire or invest or instruct. Clearly, a single book could be read once to fulfill any one of these intentions and then returned to the classroom library for students to read independently. But the books we think of as Best Friend Books, that small collection of carefully selected titles we will revisit again and again, are ripe with potential for all three of these intentions. It is easy to imagine the first read, a nonstop, start-to-finish "movie read," presented with the intention of inspiring students to explore that particular title, other titles by the same author, other titles in the same genre, or ones that share the same theme. But that same Best Friend Book can be revisited on another day with a focus on how the writer reveals the character or how the writer uses text boxes or sidebars because your intention is to invest read-aloud experiences in developing that idea across two or more titles. And, of course, that same title could be revisited during a mini-lesson when you explore a single scene or one small segment of print to instruct your students on a specific teaching point.

Selecting and Using Best Friend Books

"Neither poverty nor a thousand misfortunes should deprive any child of a book, because books DO change lives. They did mine."

—F. ISABEL CAMPOY, PROFESSOR AND POET

It seems quite simple, really. If we want children to *desire* the ability to read well, we *inspire* them by inviting them in. We read to them, showing our sheer delight in the act of reading. We read to them, letting them hear the sound effects in the background of our minds, the voices of the characters lifting up off the pages, the very mood of the text in the tone and intensity of our voices. We control the most basic elements of a read-aloud with our human voice—tone, pacing, intensity, and mood. We let our children live alongside characters in books. We let them investigate the habitats of polar bears and explore hot, dry desert terrain. We let them stand alongside children facing bigotry in the Jim Crow South. We let them know the sting of bullies. We let them know the strength of standing tall and facing a challenge. We take them into the celebrations of another culture. We let them laugh with delight at the antics of a favorite character. We show them two perspectives on the same news event. We lead a great discussion as a reaction to a letter to the editor. We launch a new study from the questions raised by responses to a book on bats. We read to them. We *read aloud to them*, and we do so with carefully thought-out *intentions*. We let them see, experience, live through the freedoms and thrills and satisfaction a reading life can provide.

When we read aloud to inspire, our expectations of students are simple and direct. We want nothing more than to pique their interest, to spark a desire, to entice them to read. Our ultimate goal is that they fall in love with language and books, that they lust after language and books and reading as they will later lust after driving. Therefore, any intentional read-aloud designed to inspire would not ask students to answer a set of questions, give a retelling, unpack meaning, host a conversation, define vocabulary, write a character sketch, or compare or contrast anything. None of that would follow a read-aloud to inspire our students. Rather, we want to leave them laughing. We want to see their eyes welling up with tears in those poignant moments in the text. We want them holding their breath as suspense builds. We want to leave them begging: "One more book . . . ," "Five more pages . . . ," "Just one more paragraph, please, we have to know what happens. . . . " We want them talking about the book as they are walking to lunch, and when scurrying about on the playground or boarding the bus. We want the language lingering in their heads. We want the reading to have lasting power. We want them to want reading for themselves.

So when we read aloud with the intention to inspire, we will naturally rely on favorite authors and beloved titles that we have fallen in love with over and over. One thing is sure here: Our passion and zeal for the act of reading and for the language being read must be evident. Then we move on to introduce our students to new authors and illustrators, broadening the set of options, widening the net for matchmaking, so to speak. We are careful to introduce new genres and expose our students to a range of themes, styles, and topics. We select material for read-aloud experiences knowing that our students have varied interests and backgrounds that will influence their attractions to reading. When reading aloud with the intention to inspire,

> *"It is not enough to simply teach children to read; we have to give them something worth reading. Something that will stretch their imaginations—something that will help them make sense of their own lives and encourage them to reach out toward people whose lives are quite different from their own."*
>
> **—KATHERINE PATERSON**

we may select a short poem about a baseball game, a feature article about changes at the park, or a letter to the editor protesting a plan to clear the woods behind the school to make a space for a fast-food restaurant. We may select a chapter book that will be shared in several installments across two weeks. We may select student-authored material or perhaps something we have written. We may select a collection of riddles and jokes. We may select a set of stories about school. The point is, we select *what* we read with the same intentionality we follow in selecting *why* we read. In fact, *what* we read aloud is inextricably connected to *why* we read aloud.

What Are the Qualities of Best Friend Books?

We all have favorite books that we love to share with students. But a Best Friend Book is more than just a favorite read-aloud. As teachers, we each have books that we read to our students for the sheer joy of it. We have others we use to introduce a topic or launch a unit of study. Those are wonderful tools for our teaching and serve an important purpose in our students' development. However, a Best Friend Book is something more. We choose a BFB because it has depth and breadth that enables us to return over and over as we unearth the nuances of meaning, the subtleties in language, the layers of characters and their motivations, and more.

A BFB is a trusted text that we carry in our hearts and heads as we move about the room from writer to reader, conferring about an array of topics from developing a character to interpreting a text. It is more than a read-aloud to spark interest in memoir or launch a study of realistic fiction. It is more than an excellent text to explore how transitions work to move the reader from scene to scene. It is more than the best example of how to embed definitions of topic-specific words. It is a rich, robust, deep text that allows us to see more each time we visit, to gain deeper insights, and to come away knowing more about ourselves as readers and writers.

SPOTLIGHT ON LESTER VIDEO

What Are the Qualities of a Best Friend Book?

scholastic.com/URAResources

Creating a Classroom Collection of Best Friend Books

When all the members of the classroom share deep and intimate knowledge of a small collection of books, a new level of communication about reading and writing becomes possible. For example, if everyone in the class is very familiar with the book *Apt. 3* by Ezra Jack Keats, I can refer them to a particular scene where the hall light is broken. If in one of our visits we reread that scene and delve into the reasons Keats may have included that detail, we will have a deeper understanding of the use of specific detail. Following that epiphany, I will be able to sit next to any young writer in the class and ask, "So where is your 'hall light' detail in this piece?" and every writer in the room will know what I mean.

When all the members of the classroom share deep and intimate knowledge of a small collection of books, a new level of communication about reading and writing becomes possible.

Visiting a small collection of Best Friend Books many times allows us to delve into small details during each visit, resulting in deeper insights than we will have with other books in our classroom library. We can discuss how an author most effectively reveals the characters and point to examples. We can identify where the tension builds and talk about how the author makes that happen. We can delve into how the writer used a particular craft move in an attempt to persuade the reader. Our BFBs will be the books we carry in our hearts and in our heads each time we engage in a conversation about our reading or writing. Our insights about these books become a reading lens for us as we approach new texts and a writing lens for us to plan our own writing. BFBs become a part of us; we carry them with us as we move through the grades.

Possibilities for Grouping Read-Aloud and Best Friend Books

When we gather books for reading aloud to invest time, language, and conceptual information, we may group them around the following:

AUTHOR STUDY. A collection of books written by one author, selected for a close examination of the writer's style.

GENRE. A collection of books from the same genre selected to explore the parameters of the genre. This may lead into a unit of study in writing or reading workshops.

TEXT STRUCTURE. A collection of books selected to demonstrate one or more ways of organizing texts or to demonstrate selected craft techniques in writing.

TOPIC. A collection of books selected to establish background, build vocabulary, develop concepts, or otherwise create a framework for deeper study of a specific topic, such as the Underground Railroad, the water cycle, or bats.

THEME. A collection of books selected to broaden or deepen an understanding of a selected theme, such as friendship, community, bullying, conservation, immigration, social justice, and so on.

I recommend five fiction and five nonfiction titles for a collection of Best Friend Books. You can find printable graphic organizers for Possibilities for Grouping Read-Aloud and Best Friend Books and Guiding Questions for Selecting Best Friend Books at scholastic.com/URAResources. Guiding questions for selecting titles include:

- Does this book have adequate depth and substance to warrant visiting again and again?

- Do the language and art offer various lenses for several visits?

- Are the literary elements or text features strong enough to support focused exploration?

- Is the information accurate and engaging?

- Does the writer employ craft techniques to support the reader's construction of meaning?

- Does the use of text features (when included) clarify, elaborate, and/or extend information?

- Will this book serve as a lens for thinking about reading other books?

- Will this book help build reading insights that can be "flipped" into writing opportunities? See *Writers ARE Readers* (Laminack and Wadsworth, 2015).

SPOTLIGHT ON LESTER VIDEO

How Do You Build a Powerful BFB Collection?

scholastic.com/URAResources

Why Limit Best Friend Collections to Ten Books?

Read-aloud experiences are essential in the development of readers and writers. There is no limit to the number of books, stories, poems, articles, and other texts that I'd recommend for typical read-aloud experiences across the day. However, the idea behind selecting a small collection of books designated as Best Friend Books moves beyond the typical read-aloud in both intention and exposure. Since the intention with BFBs is to become intimately familiar with each book, the number of books has to be small. I believe five fiction and five nonfiction is sufficient without becoming a burden. I find it is unrealistic to expect students (or teachers) to be that intimately familiar with more than five fiction and five nonfiction books. Remember, the intention is that these books will live in the hearts and minds of each student in the classroom community. We are working to develop a level of familiarity that enables us to carry these books with us into our reading and writing lives, to call upon them as trusted mentors, and to tag them as we confer with one another across the year. Each of the five fiction books will be introduced via the uninterrupted "movie read" and will then be revisited several more times across the year. The five nonfiction books may be read in segments due to the length or density of information or chunking of text by topic. Some of them may be read in one visit while others may be presented in small segments. In any case, the first visit with a selection will be an uninterrupted read followed by an opportunity for students to reflect and pose questions.

WHAT THE RESEARCH SAYS

When it comes to genre, form follows function. As Nell Duke and her co-authors remind us (2012), "Every text is meant to do something for someone— an advertisement to convince us to buy something, a nutrition label to tell us what a food product contains…. Today, many scholars see genres primarily as defined by their purposes"—what is the primary aim of the text? What is it trying to accomplish? Answering these questions will help us understand why the writing appears in a particular form or format. (Duke et al., 2012)

Assigning Best Friend Books to Specific Grade Levels

When selecting the titles for a BFB collection, I am conscious of the substance of the book. That is, I want to make sure each title has layers we can peel back as we visit it again and again over time. But I also want to connect with the emotional and developmental range of students. I have taken books with me into classrooms knowing the book would make a great read-aloud only to discover that I needed to move it up to use with an older group if I wanted to read it again the next day and go deeper. As you read, make note of what you believe you'd like to lead students to notice and think about. Chances are that your first reading or two will fill a couple of pages in your notebook. After those initial readings, take a moment to review your notes and cluster what you have noticed.

In fiction these may include:

- character(s)
- setting
- challenge or problem
- attempts to reach a solution
- solution
- craft in language
- structure

In nonfiction these may include:

- concepts
- topic-specific vocabulary
- text features
- transitions between topics
- craft in language
- accuracy of information
- author's perspective

Then reread with only one of those in mind. For example, as you read a third time, think about the main character (MC) only. Notice how the MC is revealed. Is it through dialogue or action? Is it through what others say about the MC? Is it through how the MC reacts to problems or opportunities? Is it through interior monologue or through what other characters are thinking? Do the actions and comments of other characters serve as a window into the MC? As you read with the MC as your focus, think about how you'd describe that character. Think about appearance and demeanor, and mannerisms and behaviors. As you think about the type of person the MC is, consider these two questions:

1) What is your evidence?

2) How did the writer and/or illustrator reveal this?

Now you'll have a deeper understanding of character development. That insight creates a framework for you to lead your students to do the same as you read and revisit books in your BFB set.

Finding the best fit involves taking the time to read and reread the book several times, shifting your focus each time. Approaching the story with a new lens each time focuses your thinking and helps you notice nuances you may miss otherwise. Consider repeating the fiction example above with the lens focused on a secondary character, or zooming in on how tension is built in the plot, or thinking carefully about how the setting is integrated into the story. You can find a printable

WHAT THE RESEARCH SAYS

The research makes clear that the benefits of rereading are numerous and potent. What do we know about rereading as an instructional strategy? Consider these studies, both golden oldies and current:

- **Rereading helps students develop a deeper understanding of what they have read. (Roskos & Neuman, 2014)**

- **Rereading helps students read with greater fluency, allowing them to give more attention to making sense of what they have read. (Rasinski, 2010)**

- **Rereading helps students develop greater accuracy in reading. When students reread, words that they may have struggled to decode on a first reading become increasingly easier to parse. (Samuels, 1979)**

- **Rereading leads to much deeper and more sophisticated discussions and should be a common instructional strategy in every classroom. It's an opportunity for children to understand how text is constructed and the array of decisions every writer must make as he or she uses print to convey a particular set of understandings. Rereading not only builds students' confidence as readers, but also builds their capacity to read deeply, responsibly, and with full joyful engagement. (Beers & Probst, 2012)** graphic organizer for Assigning Best Friend Books to Specific Grade Levels at scholastic.com/URAResources.

Let's explore one other example and consider how we would revisit a story with setting in mind. Let's assume for this example that the story is set in an apartment building in a city and it is a gloomy, rainy day. As we read, let's notice how the rain impacts the story. Does it limit the characters in any way? Does it cause them to stay indoors? Does it affect the mood in the story? Does it have any bearing on the mood of the characters? How is the plot dependent upon it being a rainy day? Would the characters have made other choices in different weather? Would the story have been different if the weather had been mild and sunny, or cold and in the middle of a blizzard? How does the placement of characters in an apartment building impact the plot and the characters? Would the story have been different if the same characters lived in a two-story farmhouse in the rolling hills of eastern North Carolina? Does the apartment building offer opportunities that would be unavailable in the suburbs? As you read, tune in to the idea that the writer made conscious choices about every nuance. Each decision has an intended impact.

The point here is to be conscious of what it is you want to unearth in your visits with each BFB. Reading and revisiting a text many times, revisiting each time with a specific lens, making notes of insights and evidence and technique, and then reflecting on what you glean will help you realize the depth of work each book can support. These insights will guide you in deciding which books best fit the age/grade level.

CAN A BEST FRIEND BOOK "WORK" AT MORE THAN ONE GRADE LEVEL?

Most of us can tell stories of some book or another that somehow became the "exclusive property" of a particular grade level. I recall leading a workshop for a district several years ago. There was an emphasis on moving toward a literature-based model of reading instruction and the conversation shifted to whether a grade level could lay claim to a particular title. There was a great deal of discussion about *Charlotte's Web*, and it became quite clear that in this district, fourth grade had laid claim to the book. Teachers had spent a great deal of time creating files of questions and activities for students

SPOTLIGHT ON LESTER VIDEO

Can a Book Be Used as a BFB Across Grade Levels?

scholastic.com/URAResources

to respond to after reading each chapter. There were haystacks to be made from Chinese noodles and melted butterscotch chips. There were spider webs to be woven from black yarn and coat hangers. Messages were written on those webs in Elmer's glue and sprinkled with silver glitter. The culminating event was a play performed at night for the parents and community. Needless to say, *Charlotte's Web* was a big deal in fourth grade. From the conversation, it became clear that some second-grade teachers had been reading *Charlotte's Web* aloud to their class. As you might imagine, this was not well received and I was being asked whether it was appropriate. Well…don't ask me unless you want to know what I think!

Here's what I said: Let's just think about this. Currently, *Charlotte's Web* is a cultural event, a rite of passage, and a marker of being in fourth grade. A great deal of time is devoted to that whole event. A *great deal* of time. It appears the concern is that having a second-grade teacher read the book aloud will "ruin" it for all fourth graders. Hold that thought for a moment. Have any of you, as adults, ever read the same book twice? Ever paid money to watch the same movie more than once? Ever stood in line to see the same play a second time? I suspect the answer to that is yes. And I suspect the reason is because the book, movie, or play was so compelling and complex that you simply couldn't take in all of it in one visit. I suspect that the second time through you actually noticed more, tuned in differently, and relished particular moments that you missed the first time.

> "*One cannot read a book: one can only reread it. A good reader, a major reader, an active and creative reader is a rereader.*"
>
> **—VLADIMIR NABOKOV**

I suspect you needed that first time to provide a context, a road map, that helped you fit all the bits together and to "get" the story. I suspect the second or third visit was when you were able to take in the nuances and understand more deeply, to feel and think and relish the delight of it all.

So let's think about *Charlotte's Web*. It's a beautiful story that holds such meaning for readers. Let's imagine that a second-grade teacher reads it aloud a bit at a time over several days in the classroom. What lingers with the seven- to eight-year-old? Maybe it's the magic of a spider that can write. Maybe it's life on the farm. Maybe it's more. But later, two years later, a fourth grader picks up that book and reads it independently. That fourth grader will read, think, reflect, and loop back in the text. That fourth grader will recall and notice and chuckle at something that may have been misunderstood in second grade. That fourth grader will come to the end of the book and think about friendships and choices. Now fast forward. That same child is now an adult—let's say 47. Now at 47, an old tattered copy of *Charlotte's Web* turns up in the back of a closet. An afternoon is spent sitting with that old treasure (and maybe a glass of wine). The 47-year-old reaches the last page and sits quietly as tears well up. The 47-year-old says nothing but sits there thinking about the power of unconditional love and marvels at the fact that it had not been noticed all those years ago.

You see, the book never changed. Not one dot on a single *i* has changed on a single page. The reader changed. The reader had life experiences, developed new concepts, misplaced trust, fell in love, lost friends, and simply lived all those years between visits with that book. Each time that reader came back to *Charlotte's Web,* the book sat waiting. Each time that reader came back, the book held the same potential. Each time that reader came back ready for more of what the text always held.

So it is my view that no book is the exclusive property of a single grade level. We must recognize that every book stands ready and makes the same offering to every reader who comes to the pages. Only those readers who come again and again will ever walk away with the fullness of what is offered, whether it is a novel, a picture book, fiction, poetry, information, or an essay. All that to say, yes, one book can become a BFB in more than one grade level. If this is the case, the challenge is for the teacher, not the child—the teacher should know the book and what it has to offer, and know the children and what they are ready to take away.

WHAT THE RESEARCH SAYS

The relation each text has to the texts surrounding it is often known as *intertextuality*. Readers build understanding as they draw information from a range of texts. Reading multiple texts across the same theme, topic, genre, or issue automatically fosters close reading and deepens and refines subject knowledge. As noted by renowned literacy researcher Peter Johnston: "To understand a text deeply, we need multiple perspectives. To understand a subject, idea, or concept more deeply, we need multiple texts because each text offers another author's perspective on the subject." (2009)

As readers finish one book in the set, they are better prepared for reading and understanding the next book in the set—and so on. Each book builds on the last. Plus, when students read across a set of related books, they inevitably notice the similarities and differences in how texts are crafted. Subtle differences across texts that might have escaped a student's notice if he or she approached each book as a singular read—including text structure and features, vocabulary, and presentational formats—come into sharp focus as students concentrate on reading and discussing a set of related texts. (Fountas & Pinnell, 2006, 2017; Beers & Probst, 2017; Scharer, 2018; and Walther, 2018)

Building Students' Connections to Best Friend Books

It is very likely that your best friends cross your mind when you are away from one another. You may hear a song and be reminded of a trip you took together. You may be shopping and notice something that person would like. You may be reading and run across a phrase your best friend says all the time. You may be pouring a cup of coffee and realize the mug was a birthday gift from that friend. Little things spark your memory and cause you to think of those people who are dear to you. That may prompt you to make a call or send a text or plan an outing. We want to ensure that our students are thinking of BFBs between visits as well.

Here's what I do. Let's assume I've read *Sheila Rae the Brave* by Kevin Henkes. After the first uninterrupted read, I pause for a few seconds and hover in silence with the story. I say something like, "I know this book is about Sheila Rae and she was certainly brave, but I'm still thinking about her little sister, Louise. I'm going to think about Louise for a while before we visit this book again."

Then, after the book is closed and returned to the BFB collection, I will pause at some random moment later that day and at a couple of other times in the next couple of days and say something like, "I'm thinking about *Sheila Rae the Brave* again. She did lots of things to show how brave she was. I need to visit that book again and notice what she thinks it means to be brave." Or, "I was just thinking about Louise. She certainly admires her big sister, Sheila Rae. I remember when I was little, I thought my big brother could do anything. When we visit that book again, I'm going to notice how Louise admires Sheila Rae and learns from her."

If the read-aloud had been a nonfiction text, let's say *Mummies* by Elizabeth Carney, after the first uninterrupted read, I pause and sit with the book for a moment and say something like, "I learned a lot of new information about mummies. I need to think about it for a while before we visit this book again." Later in the day I may mention some random fact of interest or bring up a topic-specific term used in the book or mention a text feature that was helpful. Then I would comment how that makes me even more eager to revisit this book with more careful attention.

The intention here is to model the notion that a text lingers in your thinking well after the last word is read and the cover is closed. I want to prompt the students to think about characters and ideas and issues and topics and text features and vocabulary; I want to plant the notion that readers think about stories and question ideas and generate questions after reading. I want to model this notion and demonstrate how this leads us back to revisit a book with a fresh focus.

Creating a "Buzz" Around Best Friend Books

A Best Friend Book lingers with us after the first visit. It whispers to us and beckons us to return. First impressions are important. Make sure you are thoroughly familiar with the book before you share it with your class. Read it aloud for yourself a few times to find those spots where you need to slow the pace or drop your voice to a whisper. Get to know the characters, content, and language well enough so that the tone of your voice will convey the appropriate tone and evoke the mood or feeling of the text. Immerse yourself in the book so you will be aware of the subtle (and not so subtle) ways the author builds tension or creates interest and let your voice signal that as well. Spend time with the illustrations or photographs or text features and explore how details in these supports open avenues to understanding for the reader.

Then, when you are ready to present the book for the first time, do it with a bit of ceremony. Let your students know this book is one that you hold dear and that you can't wait to share with them. Create a "buzz" around the book. Be clear that this first read is about understanding the text and meeting the characters or getting acquainted with the information and vocabulary. Let students know you all will be visiting this book again and again across the year and that you will have several opportunities to look closely at every detail.

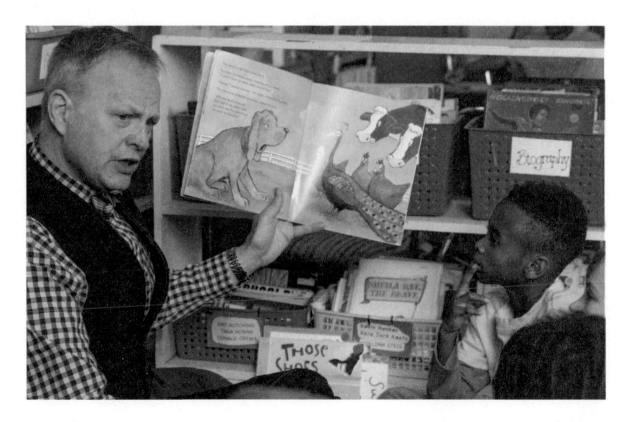

Introducing Your BFB Collection to Students

Developing a close friendship takes time. It takes intention and it takes being together. If we want our students to develop this level of understanding and familiarity with a small collection of books, we must have a plan.

Begin as you would if you were introducing two of your friends who don't already know each other. That assumes you believe the two will "hit it off" and find one another interesting. In the first meeting you are the one holding most of the knowledge; you know something about each of the other two people. Likewise, when introducing your students to a BFB for the first time, you will already have insider knowledge of the book and of the children. You'll know that the tension is going to build on the third page. You'll know that the sister is going to get homesick and come home from camp a week early. You'll know that the little brother will act as if this spoils his summer, but he secretly delights in having the sister home again. You will know that an engaging detail is lying in wait in the second paragraph under the third heading. You will know that this writer will slowly pull your students in and leave them fascinated with spiders. And you'll also know that in your classroom Nico is missing a sister who went away to college this year. You will know that Nico thinks every spider is a mortal enemy and will be surprised by what Gail Gibbons has to teach him. You'll know that Maya is an only child who wishes she had a sister. And you'll know the way the author uses details to build tension is the very thing Anthony is trying to do in his draft. You are the matchmaker in this scenario, so you begin slowly and plan for several future meetings to nurture the friendship you are certain will develop.

> *"Immature poets imitate, mature poets steal."*
>
> —**T.S. ELIOT**

The Impact of Best Friend Books on Students' Reading and Writing

We don't expect big changes to occur rapidly. We take our time getting to know each one of the BFBs. We understand that each revisit with a BFB helps us to gain deeper insights about the character or the development of the story, but it also causes us to look at other stories and characters with new insights and fresh questions. Soon we begin to notice students bringing their BFB insights to new titles. We hear it in their comments while conferring. We hear it in their conversations with peers about books. We see it in written responses and notice it in the questions and conversations that emerge from other read-aloud experiences.

Then we carry those ideas forward into our writing work. As readers, we have noticed and wondered and questioned as we revisit our BFBs. We have explored characters and thought about how the writer helped us know them. We have examined their challenges, their motivations, their personalities, their strengths, and their flaws. We have examined the setting and delved into how it impacts the characters and the plot. We have thought about the decisions the writer made to set those ideas in motion. We have discovered the places where the tension builds, and we have made note of how the writer made that happen. We have examined the use of dialogue, the placement of specific details, the choice of a particular concrete noun, and numerous other things in our quest to know this story more intimately. We have explored the author's note in several different books. We have broadened our topic-specific vocabulary and have uncovered several ways writers can teach readers about the meanings of those words. We have discovered that a text box can be included for several different reasons. We have found that back matter matters. We leave the experience knowing more about several topics, but more important, we leave with greater understanding of how to read and write. And through all of this we have always looped back to thinking about what the writer (and/or artist) did to set it up for us.

HOME VISIT

Connect With Families!
scholastic.com/URAResources

At school, your students have connected to their Best Friend Books in multiple ways; now invite them to connect their Best Friend Books to their families. Download some simple talking points families can use to guide their BFB conversations at home.

So now we bring new insights into our writing work. We know how story works and how characters are developed. We understand how to build tension and, more important, we know why it needs to happen. We have insights into how pacing works, how transitions take us from one scene to the next and link all the pieces together. We actually think about setting and recognize whether the plot is dependent on certain weather conditions or a particular geography. We understand how dialogue is more than just talk between characters—we know that it can reveal motives and attitudes and emotions, and introduce characters that never make an appearance in the story. We know how to introduce a topic and organize information into manageable chunks. We understand the function and application of headings and can use them to stay focused in our writing. We have gained insight into how text features can be used to support and elaborate details to clarify and extend our intentions. When we encounter a chart or text box we have an understanding of the range of functions it can serve. When we see bold print, italics, or a shift in the size of the font, we know to read carefully to find out what the writer is attempting to signal us to notice. We know things about our BFBs that can inform our own decisions as we sit down to plan our next writing project.

Closing Thoughts

Dear friends are with us always. We know that our best friends "have our backs" and will come to our aid in a flash if we need them. In that way, our best friends are always part of us; they are with us even when we can't see them. Our Best Friend Books are like that. They are on reserve, waiting in our minds and hearts. We may even forget they are there until we sit down to read a new book or plan our next writing. Then those BFBs begin to emerge. As we meet new characters, we are reminded of a BFB character. When the plot takes an unexpected twist, we grin and think of how that happened in one of our BFBs. When we begin to read the dialogue between two characters and discover there is a third character we have not yet met, we just chuckle. We know how that works because one of our BFBs did that as well. Yep, those BFBs are there waiting to come to our aid.

Getting to Know a Best Friend Book: The First Visit

"The first reading of a book is a gift we unwrap together. The magic of that moment happens only once."

—LESTER L. LAMINACK

The first read-aloud of a Best Friend Book is a gift. Like any gift, the excitement and joy of unwrapping it to discover the treasure inside is something that can't be relived. Take care with this privilege, do it slowly, and let your students relish the language and the unfolding of the text. There is great satisfaction in the opportunity to come to know a book slowly. Remember, each Best Friend Book will be visited again and again, so there is no need to rush. Don't be in a hurry; you want your Best Friend to make a good first impression.

Starting With the "Movie Read"

I like to call the first read-aloud the "movie read." Imagine that your friend invites you over to watch a movie. Your friend says, "Oh gosh, I love this movie. It's one of my favorites, I know you will love it, too." You agree. When you arrive your friend offers snacks and beverages, reaches for the remote, and turns the TV on. You settle back on the sofa eagerly awaiting the movie. Your friend presses pause and turns toward you. "Now, before I start the movie there are a few things I should explain. The plot is rather complex so I'll explain how it goes before we watch. Also, you need to know there are some unusual special effects in the second scene. Since you don't go to movies as often as I do, you may not get what's going on. . . ." For the next few minutes your friend continues telling you "what you need to know" so you will understand the movie. You smile and nod and hope the movie will start soon. Finally, the movie is running and you are about 15 minutes in. You are engaged with the story line and your friend presses pause. "Hey, this is the part where those special effects get tricky. Did you notice where…? So, tell me what you think is happening so far. Are you getting it?" You find this disconcerting, even a bit aggravating. But you respond and engage in the conversation. About the time you find yourself getting involved in the ideas of this conversation, your friend says, "OK, let's get back to the movie." And with a press of the play button you find yourself trying to switch from your thoughts about the special effects and the way they impact the plot back to the unfolding story on the screen.

This whole scenario would be absurd to most adults.

When you are going to watch a movie you typically buy your ticket, enter the theater, and watch from start to finish without interruption. There are no commercial

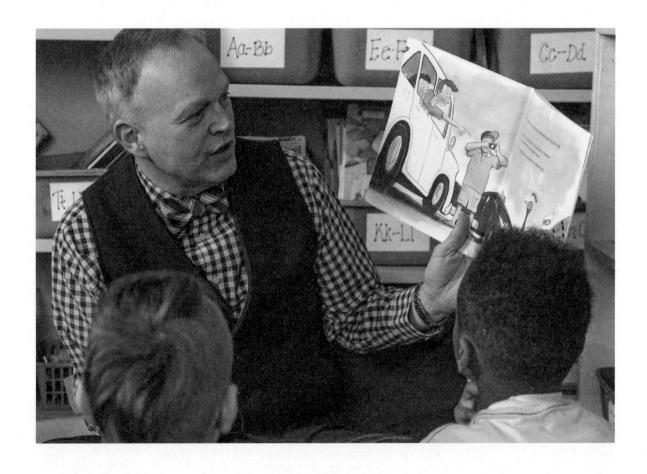

breaks. There is no pause button. There is no one on the speaker stopping the movie at critical spots to quiz you, nudge your conversation, interrupt the flow of the story, or clarify anything that might not be clear. That first viewing of a movie is an experience in which you are focused on getting the big picture even though you attend to various details and aspects as the story unfolds. If you are watching with a friend, you may leave the theater in silence as you both reflect, or you may dive into a conversation the second it ends. You and your friend will likely agree on much. However, chances are there will be differences in what you notice, and you will likely have a few differences in your interpretations of some aspects of what you saw. The conversation that ensues will likely prompt you to rethink, perhaps even revisit, the movie a second time.

I believe in the power of interactive read-aloud experiences. I have seen powerful insights develop through that experience. However, I firmly believe that every read-aloud experience does not need to be an interactive read-aloud. These Best Friend Books are titles you and your students will visit many times across the year. The first visit, then, is devoted to getting acquainted. The intention of this first visit is to capture interest and attention, to leave the students wanting to talk and ask questions and look back to check on something. In short, the purpose is to entice them to want more. You want them to think, reflect, and talk with each other. You want them to discover the feeling of lingering with the language and thinking about characters after the book is closed. You want them to notice what the writer is doing and how that helps them construct meaning.

Our friendships develop in a similar way. When you meet a new person who piques your interest, you are likely to plan another visit or outing together. It would be rare to leave that second meeting knowing everything there is to know about your new friend. But you are likely to leave knowing more, knowing something new. This may lead to more and more time together, and each visit will bring new insights, new questions, and new wonderings as your friendship blossoms over time.

Two things are significant here. First, the friendship (the bonds and depth of caring) does not happen all at once. Rather, it takes time for this to develop. It unfolds slowly and organically, arising from common interests and communication. And secondly, in a friendship there is something that draws you in, something that pulls you toward a second

SPOTLIGHT ON LESTER VIDEO

Your First Visit With a Best Friend Book: The "Movie Read"

scholastic.com/URAResources

and third and fourth meeting to spend more time together. Perhaps the process of gradually coming to know someone is part of what pulls us to return and spend more time together. Perhaps the process of an emerging friendship is rewarding in itself.

Let's consider this idea with a carefully selected set of books—say five fiction and five nonfiction for each grade level. Think about a set of books you know very well, books you have turned to over and over again across the year. Think of a single title you bring into your classroom community every year. Think of that title as a best friend who has been with you for several years. So this year you are going to introduce this title as you would introduce a best friend.

The first visit is an opportunity to get acquainted, so I say something like this:

I have a book I can't wait to share with you. I have loved this book for a long time and I think you will love it, too. [Hold the book facing the students.] *It is called* [say the title] *and it is written by* [say the author's name] *and the illustrator is* [say the illustrator's name]. *This is one of my Best Friend Books, and we are going to visit with this book several times this year. Soon each of us will know this book like we know our own best friends. So, for this first visit we can take our time and enjoy every word. Today, I'll read from the first page to the last without stopping, just like going to a movie.* [Read the book.]

Of course, each BFB will have a personality of its own. The tone and mood will be a bit different for each title. In the fiction titles the characters will be developed in a variety of ways, and in the nonfiction titles the topics will unfold and the information will accumulate in various ways from book to book. Read each book carefully before you share it with your class. Read it aloud a few times, and find the rhythm and shifts in intensity that set the mood of the book. Let your voice reflect the tone of the narrator and the personality of each character. Note the shifts in emotion, and echo those in your voice as you read. In nonfiction note the places where new ideas are introduced and adjust your pacing to allow students time to process. When I'm reading nonfiction aloud I try to keep in mind the narrator voice on the Discovery Channel. Think of that even pace, a serious, but not ominous tone, never rushed and always deliberate. This first read-aloud is important. It is the introduction to a new best friend.

> **"***From my own experience I realize that the literature I heard, rather than read, as a child resonates again and again in my memory whenever I sit down to write.***"**
>
> **—MEM FOX**

Examples of First Visits With Best Friend Books

On the following pages, you can find examples for how you can introduce students to Best Friend Books for the first time. Remember that the goal is to not interrupt the experience of the book during this first "movie read," but to know that you'll be revisiting the book again and again in the coming days, weeks, or months, and will have plenty of time for further study and inquiry.

FIRST VISIT WITH BEST FRIEND BOOK (KINDERGARTEN)

Owen, written and illustrated by Kevin Henkes

CHARACTERS

- **Owen**—young boy (mouse) who is about to enter school (main character)
- **Mom**—caring and supportive
- **Dad**—caring and supportive
- **Mrs. Tweezers**—adult neighbor who offers advice to Owen's parents (catalyst for tension)

SETTING

Owen's home and yard

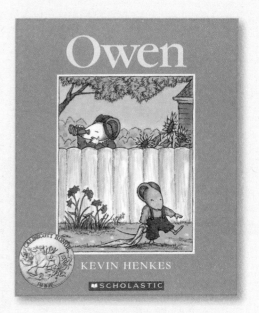

PLOT

Owen has a favorite blanket (Fuzzy) that he takes EVERYWHERE. Owen will start school soon. Fuzzy is getting worn, and his neighbor, Mrs. Tweezers, suggests several times that Owen is just too big for the blanket. Mrs. Tweezers makes several suggestions for getting Owen to give it up. Though his parents try them all, none of them work. Finally, Owen's mom arrives at a solution to make a collection of handkerchiefs from Fuzzy.

PERSPECTIVE

Text is presented from the main character's perspective.

POINT OF VIEW

Third person

1 Remember this "movie read" is your first meeting with a new best friend. Just read and relish knowing you will return for a closer look and much talk. Here are a few things to keep in mind during your first read:

- Owen is a very happy child who loves his blanket.

- His parents seem totally unconcerned about his attachment to his blanket until Mrs. Tweezers starts to offer her suggestions.

- Mrs. Tweezers seems to be a bit of a busybody. She has grown children and believes it is her obligation to make sure others benefit from her experience and "wisdom."

- Notice how the tone shifts slightly when Owen's parents become concerned about Fuzzy.

- Owen's parents try Mrs. Tweezers's suggestions but remain supportive of Owen. He is never pushed or forced to give up Fuzzy.

2 After reading, encourage reflection by asking students one of the following questions:

- *Which character are you thinking about right now?*

- *What are you wondering?*

- *What surprised you in this story?*

3 Over the next few days, prior to your return visit, bring up the book from time to time. You want to keep the characters and the story fresh in students' minds.

Your intention here is to model the notion that experiences with stories linger after we leave the book. You want to nudge students' thinking and spark conversation about the book between visits. Perhaps you say something like:

- *You know, when we were reading* Owen, *I kept thinking that Fuzzy was almost like Owen's very best friend.*

- *I keep thinking about Mrs. Tweezers. I'm not sure why she kept telling Owen's mom and dad to take Fuzzy away. We may need to think about that when we visit with her again.*

- *I was just thinking about Owen. I remember how the words told us how much he loves Fuzzy. As I think about that, I remember seeing things in the art. Maybe we should visit* Owen *again and look closely at those illustrations.*

FIRST VISIT WITH BEST FRIEND BOOK (GRADE 1)

Spiders, written and illustrated by Gail Gibbons

SUMMARY

This is an informational, fact-filled all-about book on spiders. The text is detailed without being overwhelming, with definitions embedded in the text and detailed illustrations. The balance between language and illustration is supportive for young readers, as is the inclusion of captions and labels that offer clarification and added detail.

TEXT FEATURES

- illustrations with labels and captions
- headings
- pronunciation guide
- directions/procedural text
- bonus information on final page

VOCABULARY

- *abdomen*
- *arachnids*
- *cephalothorax*
- *egg sac*
- *exoskeleton*
- *molting*
- *pedipalps*
- *poison*
- *silk*
- *spiderlings*
- *spinnerets*

1 Show the front cover of the book.

- *This is a nonfiction book. When we read it, we will learn some new words and new ideas. The title is* Spiders. *Think about that and take a look at the cover. What do you expect we will learn?*

- Before you read aloud, take a moment and briefly move through the pages with your students to get oriented with the text layout and features. Remind them that this is a nonfiction book and it may include features we don't usually find in fiction. As you move through, point out the text features listed on the previous page.

2 Continue looking through the book with students, pausing to review some of the features.

- *This book has a lot of information about spiders. The main text is at the bottom of each page. But each page also has an illustration, and some of those illustrations have extra information in the labels and the captions.*

- You may find it helpful to read the main text once all the way through to establish background information for the details provided in the illustrations, labels, and captions. Take this opportunity to demonstrate how to sample the text to determine how you might begin reading. Point out that a few of the illustrations have a lot of information in them (for example, the spread that compares a spider's body to an insect's body).

3 Decide how much of the text you're going to share during this first visit and read that aloud to the students.

- *These illustrations have a lot of extra information. I think we will need to look closely at those pages and spend some time there. Today, I'll read the main text at the bottom of each page so we can get the big ideas. Then we will visit this book again and take a close look at the extra information.*

- Read the main text on each page without stopping to comment. Remember, this first visit builds background information and embeds new vocabulary from the list on the previous page.

4 Find out what questions students have after reading the book.

- Invite students to share their questions with the class, jotting down the questions in a notebook. Later, you'll sort the questions by category to determine what to focus on in your return visits.

- Three possible categories of questions include:

  1. Vocabulary (What is a *spiderling*?)

  2. Background information (Can every spider bite you?)

  3. Schema/Conceptual (Why do spiders molt? Wouldn't that kill them?)

FIRST VISIT FOR BEST FRIEND BOOK (GRADE 4)

Shark Lady: The True Story of How Eugenie Clark Became the Ocean's Most Fearless Scientist, written by Jess Keating and illustrated by Marta Álvarez Miguéns

SUMMARY

Shark Lady is an accessible and engaging biography of Dr. Eugenie Clark. The text traces Eugenie's intense interest in sea life from her childhood to her now famous career. As a scientist, Dr. Clark made significant contributions to our understanding of sea life, especially sharks. The endpapers and back matter offer additional information to support the text.

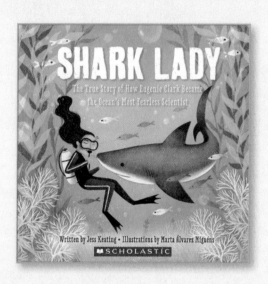

TEXT FEATURES

- illustrated endpapers with captions
- illustrations
- additional information (Shark Bites)
- important dates (Eugenie Clark Time Line)
- author's note
- bibliography

VOCABULARY

- *apex predators*
- *aquarium*
- *conveyor belt*
- *dispelled*
- *groundbreaking*
- *laboratory*
- *sanctuary*
- *zoology*

1 Show the front cover.

- *The title is* Shark Lady: The True Story of How Eugenie Clark Became the Ocean's Most Fearless Scientist. *From the title it's clear that we can expect to learn about the life and work of Eugenie Clark. We will likely find out what she did that made her famous. Think about the writer and the research she had to do. Think about the decisions she had to make about what to include in this one book. How did she decide what to leave out?*

2 Continue looking through the book with students, pausing to review some of the features.

- Before you read the text aloud, take a moment to briefly go through the pages with students to get an overview of the layout. Remind them this book is a biography. As you move through, point out the text features listed on the previous page.

- *This book has illustrations and a text layout that looks very much like a picture book, a story. We noticed a time line, a section in the back with additional information, an author's note, and a bibliography. This book is a biography, a narrative that tells us the story of one important scientist's life.*

3 Decide how much of the text you're going to share during the first visit and read that aloud to students.

- Read the text once through without pausing to explain or discuss. Save the back matter for another visit. Keep your pace steady and do not rush. If you need a model, think of the narrator voice for documentaries on the Discovery Channel (maybe *Shark Week*). Your intention here is to develop an overview of Clark's life and work and layer in new vocabulary.

4 Find out what questions students have after reading the book.

- Invite students to share their questions with the class, jotting down the questions in a notebook. Later, you'll sort the questions by category, which will help you evaluate what to focus on in your return visits.

- Three possible categories of questions include:

  1. **Vocabulary** (What is *zoology*?)

  2. **Background information** (Where is the Red Sea?)

  3. **Schema/Conceptual** (Why were people always telling Eugenie what to do and whom to be?)

FIRST VISIT FOR BEST FRIEND BOOK (GRADE 5)

Crow Call, written by Lois Lowry and illustrated by Bagram Ibatoulline

CHARACTERS

- **Lizzie**—younger of two sisters (main character)
- **Jessica**—older sister, offers a point of contrast, giving us a bit of insight into Lizzie's personality
- **Daddy**—has been away fighting in a war and feels like a stranger to Lizzie
- **Salesman and a waitress**—these secondary characters provide situations that allow us to witness Lizzie and Daddy react and interact

SETTING

A rural farming community in Pennsylvania in November 1945

PLOT

Father has been away for a long time and has returned from service in the war. Lizzie is getting reacquainted with her father and is groping toward getting to know him, even to be comfortable saying "Daddy" out loud. A hunting trip to reduce the crow population on the farm becomes the vehicle for forging trust, understanding, and communication.

PERSPECTIVE

Text is presented from the main character's perspective.

POINT OF VIEW

First person

1 *Since this is our first visit with Crow Call, I'll read it aloud from start to finish without stopping. Just listen and think, but hold your comments and questions until later. After I finish, we'll take a few moments to sit with this story and think about it before we move on to our work for the day.*

- Note this text is a memoir set in the mid-1940s when the narrator reunites with her father, who was away in the war. There is a bit of awkward searching to reconnect and find a place of comfort with her father, who has just returned.

- The narrator is a young girl (eight or nine years old). She is speaking in the present tense. Let your voice reflect her innocence and concern. This is not the exuberance of going to a birthday party. Take your time and let the budding relationship unfold as it would in real time.

- The story illustrates features from the era that surface in the art—the visit to the store where the shirt is purchased, and the breakfast at the diner. However, the heart of this story is the process of rebuilding a parent-child relationship that was interrupted by external circumstances. Let your voice convey Lizzie's initial hesitancy and uncertainty, and then her becoming more confident and comfortable with her father's presence in her life.

- Note that the father's patience, his calm and supportive manner, reveals his insights. Let your voice reflect his supportive tone.

2 As you conclude the book, close it and sit in silence for a few seconds. Remind your students that this story represents a true moment in time. Then read the author's note on the last page. Remember that this is the "get acquainted" visit only. You want your students to be eager to reflect and think and talk. Be sure to let them know you will be visiting this book again very soon. This book has depth and substance that provide opportunities for various points of entry into conversation and discussion. Pose one of the following questions and invite your students to write for two minutes in response.

- *What surprises you about this story?*
- *What would you like to go back to and explore in this story?*
- *What did you think about while listening to this story?*
- *What does this story make you wonder?*
- *Which character are you thinking about right now? What are you thinking?*

3 Over the next few days, prior to your return visit, bring up the book from time to time. You want to keep the characters and the story fresh in students' minds. You might say something like:

- *I keep thinking about Lizzie. She seems to be younger than you, maybe eight or nine, so maybe in third or fourth grade. If her father had been away in the war for a long time, I am wondering how old she was when he left. I wonder how much she remembers about him.*

- *I'm remembering the scene where Lizzie and her dad were sitting at the counter in the diner. That waitress seemed shocked when Lizzie's father ordered three pieces of pie. When we visit* Crow Call *again, let's think about all the things the father did and why.*

- *I was just thinking about the first page of* Crow Call. *I love the language on that page. Now that we have read the whole story, we will slow down and think about that page on our next visit. I think it will mean much more this time.*

- *I'm thinking of* Crow Call *again. Remember that scene where Lizzie is in the car sitting next to her father? I remember the two of them looking right out the window. I could almost feel how uncomfortable she was. When we visit* Crow Call *next, let's pause on that page and look closely at what Lizzie was thinking and feeling.*

Closing Thoughts

First impressions are important. Take the time to be prepared and know each Best Friend Book intimately before you make the introduction to your students. Trust the author and the illustrator of each book to know their audience; resist the urge to front-load meaning. Trust your teaching. You've led mini-lessons with the whole class, shared reading and guided reading lessons with small groups, and conferred with individuals. Trust your work. And finally, trust your students to enjoy the book and make meaning for themselves in this first meeting. Remember that you'll be visiting these Best Friend Books again and again. In those visits, you will have many opportunities to focus on individual elements and amplify what you feel is important. Give yourself permission to slow down and build a solid relationship between your students and each title. Remember that deep and lasting friendships are formed over time.

Building Relationships: Return Visits With a Best Friend Book

"The more we read, the more we know—and, therefore, the more expansive our capacity to comprehend."

—WALTER KINTSCH, PROFESSOR EMERITUS OF PSYCHOLOGY AND NEUROSCIENCE

After the first visit (the movie read), you will plan several more visits. As with any developing friendship, take it slowly and enjoy each visit. Remember, there is no need to feel you must share every insight you have about the book, or lift out every teaching point you've unearthed, or highlight all the opportunities for inferring, or note each of the cause-and-effect links in the first and second visits.

The joy here is taking the time to discover, to delve in, and to savor the moments when students see the power of reading. Slow down and be open to the world of possibilities that will emerge. It has been my experience that each focused visit with a BFB becomes a scaffold for the next visit. The layering of insight upon insight is powerful because it comes in "bite-sized" bits that students chew on and take with them into their book clubs and independent reading and later bring to the surface in their own writing.

WHAT THE RESEARCH SAYS

Proficient reading—which entails high-level comprehension—is a complex process, involving an intricate orchestration of multiple skills, strategies, and conceptual understandings also known as *systems of strategic actions.* (Fountas & Pinnell, 2006) "Text comprehension requires the involvement of many different components, relying upon many different kinds of information and yielding complex mental representations.... However, text comprehension is not simply the sum of the activity of these various processes, but arises from their *coordinated* operation as a system." (Kintsch & Rawson, 2005) Each reader builds a system for processing texts that begins with early reading behaviors and becomes a network of strategic activities for reading increasingly complex texts. (Fountas & Pinnell, 2006, 2017; Scharer, 2018; Stephens, Harste, and Clyde, 2019)

Let's think about what happens when we revisit a fiction BFB again and again. Take a moment and turn your left hand over. Now look at your palm. You are looking at a story map. Consider this:

I like to tell students we can hold our new BFB in our hand. Then I summarize the story with these five fingers:

FINGER	TEACHER TALK	KID TALK
Thumb	Initiating event	How did it get started?
Index finger	Rising action	It's getting interesting!
Middle finger	Problem/tension/climax	Now we know the problem.
Ring finger	Solving problem/falling action	How did they try to solve it?
Pinky	Conclusion	What finally happened?

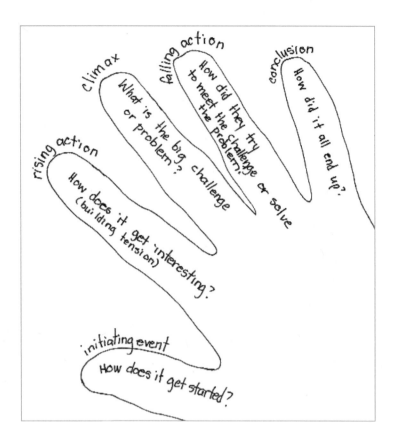

Holding the story in your hand gives you some common ground to think about the story over time. I may say something like, "I was thinking about *Peter's Chair* by Ezra Jack Keats again." I hold up my hand and look at it.

- I put my thumb up: "Peter was building towers with his blocks when the dog, Willie, ran through and knocked them down."

- I lift my index finger: "Mom reminded him to play quietly because there is a new baby in the house. Peter peeked in and saw his dad painting his old crib."

- I lift my middle finger: "Peter's feeling sad and maybe jealous."

- I lift my ring finger: "Peter takes his chair and a few things and runs away to the sidewalk with Willie."

- I lift my pinky: "Peter realizes he is too big for baby furniture and helps his dad paint the chair for Susie."

HOME VISIT

Take the Story Map Home
scholastic.com/URAResources

Download a story map for your students to share with their families—a simplified version that they can use with a well-known folktale from their own communities or with a well-known fairy tale such as *Goldilocks and the Three Bears.*

I may revisit that a few times to help set the essence of the story in their minds. Over the course of the day I may make the following observations:

- *I keep thinking about Peter. I believe he felt pretty sad for a little while. I want to revisit* Peter's Chair *and look closely at his face. Maybe that will help me know what he was feeling.*

- *I've been thinking about Peter's mother. I can't be sure if she noticed that he was feeling sad and a little jealous. Help me remember to look for that when we visit with* Peter's Chair *again.*

- *You know, I've been thinking about Peter. I think he is the kind of boy who gets upset, but he can change his mind. Let's think about what we know about Peter and try to decide.*

The intention is to model that books, stories, and characters linger in your thinking and prompt new questions and insights that lead you back to the page. Each of these "random thoughts" will be a lens for our focus in a future visit.

It is my experience that we don't take in all the nuances of a character, the elements of story, or the techniques employed by the writer in a single visit. I find it necessary to revisit as insights develop and new questions take shape. Likewise, we will have several visits with a BFB and each of them will have a specific purpose. As I plan the return visits, I explore the story with these ideas in mind:

CHARACTERS

- How many characters are in the story? Which character is the main character?
- How do the other characters help me get to know the main character?
- What is the purpose of each character in the story? How does each character contribute to the story?
- Does the main character change across the story? If so, how?
- How does the main character work to meet the challenge or solve the problem?
- How do the other characters contribute to the challenge? Solution?

SETTING

- Where is this happening? What is the physical location?
- Is it a real place? (playground, apartment) Or is it imagined in the character's mind? (an old box becomes a fort)
- What is the weather? Climate? Season? And how does this impact the characters and their decisions?
- Does the setting make a difference or is it just a backdrop for events?

PLOT

- How does the story get started?
- Where and how is tension built?
- What are the challenges or problems for the character(s)?
- What is attempted in an effort to meet the challenge or solve the problem?
- How does the plot move forward?
- How is the plot organized? What structures are employed? What impact do they have?

ART

- How do the illustrations work to reveal mood and tone?
- Do the illustrations hold a key to information not presented in the text?
- Do the illustrations parallel, support, extend, or enrich the text?
- Are there questions raised by the text that can be answered by a close examination of the art?
- What do we learn about the setting by a close examination of the art?
- What do we learn about the character(s) by a close examination of the art?

INTERPLAY (How all these factors work together to build a story)

- How are the challenges/problems linked to place, weather, or to the personality of the character?
- How do the physical location and weather conditions impact the characters?
- How do the character's fears, worries, dreams, and favorites impact the plot?
- Technique (author and/or illustrator decisions)
- Examine what the author and/or illustrator has done to lead us toward these insights.

Let's take a moment and consider what happens when we revisit a nonfiction BFB again and again.

I remind students that nonfiction may have features that we don't typically find in fiction. So I begin with a brief examination of the layout and features by slowly turning the pages and exploring what we notice. This may include the inclusion of tables, charts, maps, photos/illustrations, captions, labels, side bars, text boxes, bold print, etc. We also examine the table of contents (if one is included) and think about how the text is divided. This may happen with headings and subheadings, chapters, topics, or just with new paragraphs throughout the book.

WHAT THE RESEARCH SAYS

Frank Serafini, who is a literacy researcher as well as a picture book author and photographer, offers unique insights into the role illustrations and graphics play in today's sophisticated picture books. He writes:

> "The illustrations and visual elements contained in picture books may well be the first time young children are exposed to art and artistic techniques. Young readers are drawn into the world of reading and literature through the images and artwork contained in picture books. As readers get older, the picture books that are intended for them become more sophisticated. The media used to create the illustrations, the interplay between visual elements and written text, and the meanings and significance of the visual elements in picture books become more complex. Contemporary picture book illustrators draw upon a wide variety of artistic techniques including realism, surrealism, impressionism, cubism, and postmodernism to create their illustrations and visual elements. Making connections between the art in picture books and classic art forms and styles can increase older reader appreciation of art itself. The art contained in picture books may be a door into the world of art that older readers need to make connections to the vast array of visual elements in other texts and experience."
> (Serafini, 2008)

At times, if the book is long or dense with information, we may divide it into segments by topic (e.g., habitat, physical characteristics, diet and nutrition, mating and reproduction, unusual facts).

For each segment I ask, "What is the writer focused on here?" and "What is the big idea we can take away with us?" I find it helpful to ask students to think of a bumper sticker— a brief statement that captures the essence of the segment. These may read like summary statements, headings, entries in the table of contents, etc.

Taking these statements from each segment can help us gain access to the bigger idea(s).

When planning return visits with nonfiction texts, I focus on these ideas:

- Does the text include text features that expand or clarify information in the segment?

- Are these text features useful tools for reading nonfiction and will they serve my students as writers of nonfiction?

- Does the text have a clear organization frame that can be used to focus return visits with the book?

- Does this writer offer examples in the language, text features, and/or illustrations (or photographs) that deepen the reader's insights and understanding?

- How is topic-specific vocabulary introduced and developed?

HOME VISIT

Take Home *Owen*, *Spiders*, *The Shark Lady*, and *Crow Call*

scholastic.com/URAResources

Invite your students to introduce their families to Best Friend Books. Download a discussion guide that they can share with their families to support the conversation.

SPOTLIGHT ON LESTER VIDEO

Return Visits With *Owen* and *Crow Call* & Fiction/Nonfiction Bridge

scholastic.com/URAResources

Examples of Return Visits With Best Friend Books

Here are some examples (using the same four picture books we mentioned in the previous chapter) for topics you can focus on when you revisit your Best Friend Books with students.

RETURN VISITS WITH A BEST FRIEND BOOK (KINDERGARTEN)

Owen, written and illustrated by Kevin Henkes

LESSON FOCUS	ENGAGE STUDENTS
Identifying Qualities of the Main Character Every story has a main character, and Owen is the main character in this one. We know that he loves Fuzzy, his blanket. Let's visit again and think about other things we know about Owen.	• Owen likes to play outside. • Owen sucks his thumb. • Owen believes Fuzzy likes everything he likes. • Owen is playful (we see him in several scenes playing with Fuzzy). • Owen gets worried sometimes (blanket fairy). • Owen is clever and can solve problems (blanket fairy, vinegar trick). • Owen uses his imagination (Captain Plunger, becoming invisible).
Identifying the Main Character's Problem The main character in a story has a problem to solve or a challenge to face. We have decided that Owen's challenge is finding a way to keep Fuzzy even though the grown-ups think he is too big for a blanket. Let's visit again and notice all the ways Owen tries to keep Fuzzy.	• Owen loves Fuzzy and wants to keep him. • We see Mrs. Tweezers talking with Owen's parents several times. She tells them he is too old to play with Fuzzy. • Owen's parents try the blanket fairy, the vinegar trick, and saying no. • Owen doesn't want to give up Fuzzy.
Identifying Other Characters in a Story In addition to a main character, writers may also include other characters to help us think about important ideas. In this story, Kevin Henkes includes a neighbor named Mrs. Tweezers. In this visit, let's focus our thinking on Mrs. Tweezers. Let's think about why she is important in this story. Remember that we may need to examine the illustrations and think about the language.	• Mrs. Tweezers is peeking around the fence on the first page. She is watching Owen hold Fuzzy and suck his thumb. • On the second spread, we see Mrs. Tweezers leaning over the fence whispering to Owen's parents. She is telling them he is too old to play with Fuzzy. She tells them about the blanket fairy. • On the fifth spread, we see Mrs. Tweezers standing on flowerpots by the fence and talking with Owen's parents. She is telling them Owen can't be a baby forever and tells them about the vinegar trick.

LESSON FOCUS	ENGAGE STUDENTS
Identifying Other Characters in a Story *continued*	• On the eighth spread, we see Mrs. Tweezers at the fence. She tells Owen's parents he can't take that blanket to school, and she tells them to say no. • On the last page, we see Mrs. Tweezers at the fence. She and Owen wave to each other with their handkerchiefs. NOTE: Mrs. Tweezers helps to create tension, she helps us discover the problem, and she gives Owen and his parents something to overcome or solve.
Identifying Feelings by Looking at the Art Fuzzy was very important to Owen. Let's visit this time and think about Fuzzy. Let's think about why Fuzzy is so important to Owen. We may need to look closely at the art and look at Owen's face to find out.	• First page: We see Owen cuddled with Fuzzy. His eyes are closed and he is sucking his thumb. He looks content. • First spread: We see Owen in six small illustrations and one larger one. In each illustration, Owen is doing something with Fuzzy. They are never apart. • Second spread: We see Owen using Fuzzy to pull a little toy bird behind him. We also see Owen getting ready for bed, and he is holding Fuzzy. He looks concerned about the blanket fairy. • Third spread: Owen stuffs Fuzzy into his pajama pants so the blanket fairy can't take Fuzzy. He looks happy and relieved. • Fourth spread: Owen hides Fuzzy behind his back when his parents are talking about Fuzzy being dirty and ratty. He looks worried. Owen wears Fuzzy as a cape when he is Captain Plunger and puts Fuzzy over his head when he is invisible. He looks happy. • Fifth spread: Owen clutches Fuzzy when he has his nails trimmed, gets a haircut, and visits the dentist. His face shows concern or worry. • Sixth spread: Owen rubs Fuzzy in the sandbox and buries it in the garden to get the vinegar smell out. Owen looks playful and delighted. • Seventh spread: Owen uses Fuzzy as a flag, as a wrap, and as a wagon to pull his toys behind him. He takes a bath with Fuzzy and sleeps with it and twists it tightly while watching TV. He looks happy and content in all but one illustration. • Eighth spread: Owen holds on to Fuzzy even when he is playing in a yard filled with toys and hides his face with Fuzzy when he is crying. • Ninth spread: Owen clings to Fuzzy while his parents try to comfort him. He watches with a bit of trepidation while his mother snips and sews Fuzzy. Owen looks worried. He has tears in his eyes. • Tenth spread: Owen now has a collection of small Fuzzies, and he takes one everywhere. He looks happy.

RETURN VISITS WITH A BEST FRIEND BOOK (GRADE 1)

Spiders, written and illustrated by Gail Gibbons

LESSON FOCUS	ENGAGE STUDENTS
Gathering Key Information from Illustrations, Labels, and Captions The focus of this visit is to look closely at the function of labels, captions, and additional information in the illustrations throughout the book. The additional text here provides clarification, elaboration, and greater detail to the information presented in the main text.	For this visit, return to one spread and reread the main text as scaffolding. Then turn your attention to the support and elaboration provided by the illustration, labels, and captions. Lead your students to discover that these additional details help us to understand new ideas and vocabulary. *In nonfiction, writers sometimes give us extra information when they think we are learning something new. In this book, the writer is also the illustrator. She decides which details to include in the text and also what to add in the illustrations. That is what we do when we write, isn't it? We make the words and the illustrations. Let's take a closer look today.* Read the main text and then all the supporting text from beginning to end. Explore with students how the main text gives us general information, but the illustration gives detailed elaboration to help us understand the differences.
Organizing Information Graphically to Represent Understanding The focus of this visit is to summarize the information students have gained and put it into a chart.	*Take a moment now to think about the new ideas we have noticed in this book. Share your ideas with a partner and let's make a list of all our new insights.* As students comment, make note of their information. Lead them to make connections to what the writer or illustrator did to help them. These insights will serve you later as teaching points in writing instruction. Students may notice: • Spiders are helpful. • Spiders are arachnids and not the same as an insect. • Some spiders don't make webs. • Most spiders don't hurt people. • Spiders are web weavers. • Their webs are their homes and they catch food there. • Sometimes the female spider eats the male spider. • Spiders lay eggs, and the baby spiders are called *spiderlings*. As you draw this visit to a close, take a moment and help them notice all the new words they are using. Remind them that reading nonfiction helps us to grow our vocabulary. You and your students may choose to develop a glossary for this book.

LESSON FOCUS	**ENGAGE STUDENTS**

Exploring the Content and Purpose of Back Matter

The focus of this visit is on reviewing the back matter (Spiders…spiders…spiders!). Authors of informational texts often include a variety of features at the back of the book that clarify elements of the text, add to the content, or provide ideas for further study. For this book, point out all of the additional information readers can learn about spiders.

For this visit, focus on the last page, where the writer includes "bonus" information that your students will find interesting. You may choose to call these "fun facts" or "unusual information."

Sometimes in nonfiction, the writer has discovered extra information that doesn't fit in the main text. One way they can use this information is to make a page of interesting information in the back of the book. Let's take a look at the last page of this book and see what we notice.

Read the last page one fact at a time. You may want to pause after each one for a brief chat or comments. Try to focus on why the writer decided to save these facts for the last page.

If your students find this engaging, you may want to close by inviting them to use their new knowledge to create a "fact sheet" about spiders organized into three categories: Habitat, Diet, and Nutrition; Mating and Reproduction; and Unusual Facts.

Exploring the Craft of Nonfiction Writing

Continue exploring what writers do to engage and support readers in nonfiction. In this case, help students look at how and why writers of nonfiction choose certain words to convey information.

We are becoming experts on this book about spiders. We have explored how writers use text features in nonfiction to help readers learn more. Today, let's go back to the book and take a close look at the words. This time, as I read, I'll pause in a few spots so we can think about why writers choose certain words.

In this visit, examine each page, noting how writers use their words carefully. Point out and discuss the reason for using words like:

- "Spiders may look scary but *most* of them don't hurt people."
- "Some are so tiny that they are *no bigger than* a speck of dust."
- "Others can be *as big as* a dinner plate."

Point out the use of *some, all,* and *others* in these pages. Discuss the use of comparisons (*as big as, no bigger than*) to give relative size. Lead your students to explore why writers choose these words. As they begin to recognize the purpose of these words, reread the book and pause where you find them to discuss why the writer chose that particular word.

Note: These insights can be useful later if you refer to them in your writing instruction.

RETURN VISITS WITH A BEST FRIEND BOOK (GRADE 4)

Shark Lady: The True Story of How Eugenie Clark Became the Ocean's Most Fearless Scientist, written by Jess Keating and illustrated by Marta Álvarez Miguéns

LESSON FOCUS	ENGAGE STUDENTS
Using Details About a Time Period to Establish Historical Context Focus this visit on understanding the time period of the setting. Remember that students may lack schema and background knowledge for understanding why a woman would have met with so many obstacles.	Open this visit with the time line. The list taken as a whole offers a concise summary of the information presented in the book and offers the reader a glimpse into the typical chronological structure of biography. As you read, move between entries on the time line and the pages of the text corresponding with that time period. Pause at selected points to invite students to make note of the date, Eugenie's age, her interests, obstacles posed by cultural norms, and expectations of (or limitations placed on) women. Invite them to explore the differences between expectations and limitations that women faced then and now face. Note that this list has more meaning after the first visit with the book. You may also choose to return to this information as an organizing tool during your writing instruction when your students write biographies.
Exploring Character Traits During this visit, focus on the writer's development of Dr. Clark's interests and work with attention to character traits (e.g., curious, intelligent, focused, dedicated, hard-working, diligent).	Reread the text and pause at selected points to explore Dr. Clark's early interest in aquariums and sharks. Invite students to seek evidence of her consistent interest and growing devotion to her life's work. Pause to explore the focus of her curiosity and energy in her free time. Encourage students to make note of how Eugenie Clark's interests and habits slowly developed into the focus of her work in school and later became her life's work. Students may notice: • "…Eugenie wanted to stay at the aquarium forever….to smell the damp, salty air and stare at the glittery rainbow of fish…. watching her favorite animals…. The sharks." • "Stuffing sticky gum into her ears to keep the water out, Eugenie dove…" • "The salt stung her eyes, but she didn't want to miss a single fish." • "…sharks were only in her mind, for now. Eugenie decided to learn everything she could about them."

Gathering Key Information From Illustrations

Focus this visit on the role of the illustrations in contributing to understanding. Invite students to explore how the illustrations aid the reader's construction of meaning in situations where vocabulary and/or background information may be inadequate.

Read the text aloud, pausing at the conclusion of each spread. Invite students to notice and comment on what the illustrator has selected to depict in each scene. Explore how the illustrations provide deeper insight and greater clarity to our understanding of new information.

Students may notice:

- In the first few spreads, Eugenie is a young girl around the age of nine and the time period is the early 1930s. Note the clothing worn by people visiting the aquarium.
- Notice the illustrator included the fin Eugenie imagined as she swam underwater at the beach.
- As Eugenie reads about sharks in the library, we see sharks floating in the air to let us see what she is visualizing.
- When Eugenie attends college, we see she is the only woman in her class, and she is sitting on the front row. She is depicted as the only one taking notes.

Exploring the Craft of Nonfiction Writing

Continue exploring what writers do to engage and support readers in nonfiction. To the right are several examples of features found in nonfiction writing. Review the examples included from the book, and then have students find additional examples of these details in the book and elsewhere. Remember to explore why the writer uses this particular craft move. You can do that by thinking about how it helps you to make meaning as a reader.

Here are some things to consider:

- **Lead** (This lead places us with nine-year-old Eugenie in the aquarium. We meet the subject of the biography in her favorite environment. It foreshadows her interest, curiosity, and passion.)
- **Sensory words** ("…damp, salty air…glittery rainbow of fish." "Stuffing sticky gum into her ears…")
- **Active verbs** ("…salt stung her eyes.")
- **Specific language (concrete nouns)** ("Whale sharks. Nurse sharks. Tiger sharks. Lemon sharks. …" "…fifteen-gallon tank…")
- **Figurative language** ("Constellations of sea stars…" "…slicing through the ocean current." "It felt as big as an ocean…")

RETURN VISITS WITH A BEST FRIEND BOOK (GRADE 5)

Crow Call, written by Lois Lowry and illustrated by Bagram Ibatoulline

LESSON FOCUS	ENGAGE STUDENTS
Identifying the Main Character The narrator in *Crow Call* is Lizzie, the main character. Notice the ways we find out about Lizzie: • narration • dialogue • interior monologue/thinking • actions • reactions	Lizzie is a little timid with her dad. • She feels her father is a stranger because he has been away in the war so long. • Saying "Daddy" feels new, maybe awkward, because she has to whisper it under her breath a few times. • She is concerned about not knowing what to do when they go hunting. Lizzie wants to do things with her dad, to make him proud of her, to be like him in some ways. • She wants (and gets) a plaid hunting shirt like her dad's, even though it is a man's shirt and it is much too big. • She sits with him at the counter in the diner, her pigtails are tucked inside the collar of the big shirt, and the waitress mistakes her for a boy. Daddy winks at her, and she hopes the pigtails stay hidden. Lizzie is thoughtful, kind, and empathetic. • "I wish the crows didn't eat the crops." • "They might have babies to take care of. Baby crows." • "'Look, Daddy,' I whisper. 'Do you see them? They think I'm a crow!'… 'Listen, Daddy! Do you hear them? They think I'm their friend! Maybe their baby, all grown up!'"
Identifying Actions of Other Characters Lizzie and her father are spending a day together and getting to know each other again. On this visit with *Crow Call*, let's look closely at the father and notice what he does to help Lizzie get to know and trust him after his long absence.	• He buys her the hunting shirt she wanted, even though her sister insists it is a man's shirt and the salesman hesitates. He said, "You know, Lizzie…buying this shirt is probably a very practical thing to do. You will never *ever* outgrow this shirt." • In the diner, when the waitress mistakes Lizzie for a boy, Daddy winks at Lizzie and they play along. It's as if the two of them have a secret joke. • He orders three pieces of cherry pie, one for himself and two for Lizzie. • When Lizzie shares her concern for the baby crows that may be left behind, we gain insight into her fears of what would happen if her daddy had gotten shot in the war. Daddy explains there would be no crow babies at this time of year. • When Lizzie begins sounding the crow call, her father watches her delight and listens as she speculates that the crows believe she is one of their friends or maybe even one of their babies all grown up.

Identifying Autobiographical Details

Let's read the author's note and see what we can glean. Then let's revisit the story with that in mind.

The author's note on the last page shows Lois Lowry at the age of eight wearing the plaid flannel shirt in this story. We learn these events happened in her life in 1945. The note also reminds us of the more central message that parents and children work to build relationships and trust, and grow toward understanding one another.

Identifying Rich Language

Writers use rich language, precise nouns, and strong verbs to help us construct our understanding of the story. In this visit, let's zoom in on those places where Lois Lowry's choice of words helps us know what it was like to be in that place on that day.

Setting [time or season]

- "It's morning, early, barely light, cold for November...."
- "...the gray-green hills of early morning."
- "Grass, frozen after its summer softness, crunches under our feet...."
- "...kicking the dead leaves..."
- "It is quieter than summer."

Setting [place or location]

- "...across the Pennsylvania farmlands."
- "'Not now, Liz, not this time of year,' he says. 'By now their babies are grown...'"

Setting [weather or climate]

- "Grass, frozen after its summer softness, crunches under our feet; the air is sharp and supremely clear, free from the floating pollens of summer, and our words seem etched and breakable on the brittle stillness."
- "Our breath is steam."

Identifying Important Story Elements

The crow call and the plaid hunting shirt are very important items in this story. As we visit today, let's slow down and look closely in those places where the shirt and the crow call are featured. Let's think about why these two items are so very important in this story.

- Second spread: Note the shirt is in the scene and is described almost like a robe.
- Fourth spread: Note this scene is a flashback to explain the story of the shirt and give it greater significance.
- Fifth and sixth spreads: Here in the diner scene, the shirt hides Lizzie's pigtails and the waitress mistakes her for a boy. This becomes an inside joke between Lizzie and her father.
- Eleventh spread: In this scene, the father tells Lizzie to sound the crow call. Lizzie's comments (as narrator) give us insight into the importance she assigns to this job.
- Twelfth spread: Now many crows have gathered. The tree limbs are filled with crows like ripe fruit. Lizzie has moved away from her father and stands near the top of the hill. Her delight in this is obvious.

BRIDGE BETWEEN FICTION AND NONFICTION

The King of Bees, written by Lester L. Laminack and illustrated by Jim LaMarche

When fiction is deeply imbued with information that leaves the reader with new insights, vocabulary, and perhaps even questions about a nonfiction topic, it may be difficult to determine whether it is meant to be fiction or nonfiction. A story built on a solid foundation of nonfiction can be the doorway into deeper exploration of nonfiction, even among students who typically shy away from it. Fiction, like *The King of Bees*, can be read as

a story and discussed as a story with attention to the characters, the significance of the setting, the tension within the plot, the conflict or problem, and the process of finding resolution. It can also be revisited with attention to the information woven throughout the narrative. Returning to the story a few times to explore the literary elements will take students deeper into the craft of the writer and the nuances of the story. Coming back to the story after that with questions you'd love to ask a beekeeper builds a purpose for bringing in a small stack of nonfiction texts on honeybees. These nonfiction titles can be visited from least complex to most complex in search of answers to the questions arising from exposure to the fiction. Each nonfiction text will layer new vocabulary, refine and extend understanding, and solidify conceptual knowledge.

Let's take the time to look closely at the role of the read-aloud in a subject matter unit of study. Assume for this example that you are planning a study of honeybees in your science curriculum. You might begin by gathering the students on the carpet with a whiteboard or large chart nearby. And it would go something like this:

Each of you has heard of honeybees, right? But do you know much about them? Let's just take a minute to think about honeybees. Close your eyes if that helps you think, but focus on honeybees. I want you to search your mind and try to find all the bits of information you have tucked away in there. Hold on, I just need you to think right now about what a honeybee looks like. So get focused and try to picture a honeybee in your mind. Take a close look and try to remember all the details you can. Got it? Let's think for a moment.

Pause here for about 45 seconds.

Now turn to the person next to you and talk for 40 seconds about what you saw in your mind.

I actually time this.

Tell all the details you can and remember to listen to your partner as well.

Eyes up here, please. Talkers off. Thinkers on. Now, tell me something you heard someone else say that you think we should put on our list.

As children respond, I record what they say in blue and cluster it all together.

Note that you will likely find some responses that are factual and some that are not. List them all and make it clear that you will list anything that is believed to be true. The purpose of this list is to generate a baseline of our thinking.

Wow, we have quite a list here.

The list may include things such as *honeybees are yellow, honeybees have wings, they have stingers, their body has stripes, honeybees have three body parts,* and so on.

Now I need you to think again. Talkers off. Thinkers on. Ready? This time I want to you think, no talking yet, just think about where honeybees live. Try to picture all the places you might find honeybees if you went on a honeybee hunt. Where are those places? What does it look like there? Do the honeybees have houses, or nests, or crawl into tiny holes, or something else? Think about that for a few more seconds. When we open our eyes, I'll ask you to turn and share your thinking with the person next to you. Remember to listen and share because I'll ask you to tell me something your partner said to you. Ready? Talk with your partner for forty seconds.

This time, when you draw their focus back to you, move to a different section of the chart and write in a different color—green, for example. This way you create clusters of information that can be grouped under headings children are likely to find in an index.

Let's get your thinking listed here. I'm writing in green this time and I'll put your ideas in this corner. That way we can keep our ideas about what honeybees look like and our ideas about where honeybees live separate.

When the list is complete, you will likely have ideas such as *honeybees live in a nest, they live in those boxes on people's farms, they can live in the wall of a house, they live inside trees, they live in beehives*, etc.

Again, remember that you are getting a baseline of their perceptions. This is not about getting factual information.

Let's get focused again. Talkers off. Thinkers on. This time, I need you to think about what honeybees eat. I want you to close your eyes and think about a honeybee going to dinner. Where does the honeybee go? Do all the honeybees go together, or do they each go alone? What sort of food do they eat? Do they search for food? Where do they find it? Does the honeybee collect the food and bring it back to share? Or does the honeybee eat the food right where it is found? OK, just think for a bit.

While they are thinking, I am getting a red marker so I can continue to cluster information by heading and color to help them organize their thoughts and develop understanding during the upcoming read-aloud.

Eyes open. Turn to your partner and share your thoughts. Remember to be a good listener as well so you can report something interesting you heard. Ready? You have 40 seconds. Remember, you need to share your thinking and listen to the thinking of your partner.

I continue to stress the need to listen at this time, as most children are eager to share their own ideas. I am trying to lead them toward understanding that they can learn from listening to others. As they share their thoughts, I record them in another section of the chart using the red marker.

I continue with this, keeping the focus on habitat, mating and reproduction, diet and nutrition, physical characteristics, and movement from place to place, but I like to end this one with myths and misunderstandings about honeybees. So let's skip down to that.

Take a look at our thinking. Wow, you all have filled two chart sheets with your thoughts about honeybees! Well, I have one more thing I want you to think about before we begin to investigate. Blink twice if you are ready to think. Remember, talkers off, thinkers on. This time I want to think about all the myths and misunderstandings people tell about honeybees. Think for a minute about all the things you have ever heard about honeybees. Think about some of the things you have heard people say because they are afraid of honeybees. Think about some of the things you have heard people say because they have never even seen a honeybee. Just think about that. What are the things you've heard that you think are not really true?

Pause for a moment to let them think while you get the black marker ready.

> *Eyes open. Turn to your partner. Remember you have 40 seconds to share your thoughts and also listen to your partner's ideas.*

Remember to keep this tightly focused and quick. I try to stay within the 40 seconds so they will get to the point and stay energized about the topic. It seems to lend a sense of urgency to the whole brainstorming session.

> *So let's get your thinking listed on our chart. Ready? Let me hear some of the things you heard from your partner.*

I continue with listing out what they say, this time in black so each cluster of ideas is in a separate section and in a different color.

> *We have one more task before we begin the read-aloud and start our investigation into the life of honeybees. Let's take a look at our chart. Each section is in a different color, and each section is our thinking around one idea about honeybees. Let's look at the green section, where we were thinking about where honeybees live. Can you think of a word we might find in our science book or in other nonfiction books that means where an animal lives?*

Students will generate a list of words like *homes*, *houses*, and *shelter*. If they do not get there, I will introduce the word *habitat*.

> *So let's make a heading for the green section on this chart and call it Habitat.*

Repeat this for each section on the chart, using headings that are likely to be found in the index, table of contents, or glossary of resources you plan to use.

> *Now we have our thinking up here and ready for our study. Tomorrow we will begin with a read-aloud called* The King of Bees *by Lester Laminack, with illustrations by Jim LaMarche.*

The next day, gather your students so they can see the charts and the details in the text and the art of the book you will feature.

> *Yesterday we spent a lot of time just getting our thinking about honeybees organized on these charts. Take a look; we have thoughts on habitats and physical characteristics, diet and nutrition, mating and reproduction, movement, habits, myths and misunderstandings, and more. We did a lot of thinking, didn't we? Let's quickly read through our perceptions and thoughts before we begin the read-aloud.*

Allow time for this quick review.

Today we are going to read The King of Bees *by Lester Laminack, with illustrations by Jim LaMarche. You may remember that we read this book last week, and I told you then we would be studying honeybees. Remember, I asked you to notice words the writer used to talk about bees? As I read the book again today, I would like you to listen carefully and think about what we listed on our charts. When you hear something in the text that supports our thinking and proves that it is true, just give me a quiet thumbs-up. I'll stop as soon as I find a good place, and we can talk about what you noticed. Also listen for information that causes you to question some of our thinking. If you hear anything that makes you think our ideas might be incorrect, just let me know with a quiet thumbs-down. Again, I'll stop as soon as I find a good spot, and we will revisit and revise the chart. When we finish, we will see if we are able to fine-tune our thinking on the charts. Then we can ask better questions, and tomorrow I'll have another book that has even more information about honeybees.*

This second reading of a picture book gives them some familiar territory as we begin reading aloud to instruct—to stretch children's thinking and have them revise some of their misunderstandings and misperceptions. As you read along, there will be several places where you can pause to verify and validate the thinking they have listed on the chart. Take the time to signify that validation. I like to simply place a small plus sign to the left of the item on the list. When there is conflict between the information we are gaining from a read-aloud and the ideas we have on the chart, I prefer to signal that with a question mark. The reason for this is it calls our attention to the need for us to check our thinking as we delve into the read-alouds that will follow this one.

Let's take a look at the way our thinking was stretched by this book.

Review the chart, drawing attention to the validations and revisions.

Now that we know more about honeybees, I'm thinking we could ask some good questions to focus our investigation. Let's go back to our categories here on the chart. Shall we begin with Habitat? We found out that honeybees do prefer places that are near areas where there are lots of flowers blooming so they can find nectar. Does that leave you with any questions?

List the questions that arise from revisiting the thinking that was validated or revised and continue a similar process with each of the sections.

Tomorrow we will read another book about honeybees. It is called Bees: Let's Read About Insects *(Weekly Reader). It is more of an all-about information book. When we read it, I am sure we will find answers to some of our questions from today. I think we will also find some new information to add to our charts.*

I will continue this for two or three days, each day reading a book that is more complex, more detailed, more specific than the one before. This process allows each book to scaffold for the ones to follow and enables the students to accumulate information in layers. Each layer of information creates a base for the next, giving the students enough background to make sense of the next layer.

Here are some books you might find useful in this particular example:

- *The King of Bees* by Lester Laminack
- *Beekeepers* by Linda Oatman High
- *Bees* (Let's Read About Insects) by Susan Ashley
- *Bees!* by the editors of *TIME for Kids* with Elizabeth Winchester
- *Zoom in on Bees* by Melissa Stewart
- *Are You a Bee?* (Backyard Books) by Judy Allen and Tudor Humphries
- *Flight of the Honey Bee* (Read and Wonder) by Raymond Huber
- *The Honey Makers* by Gail Gibbons
- *Honey in a Hive* (Let's Read-and-Find-Out Science) by Anne Rockwell
- *What If There Were No BEES?: A Book About the Grassland Ecosystem* by Suzanne Slade
- *The Honeybee* by Kirsten Hall
- *The Bee Book* (DK, 2016)
- *The Bee Tree* by Patricia Polacco
- *Bee: A Peek-Through Picture Book* by Britta Teckentrup
- *Bees: A Natural History* by Christopher O'Toole
  Note: This is a large reference book with great photography.

As you read each book, you will have opportunities to model the use of an index to look for specific information, to address a question, or to return to a page to find a detail to resolve some confusion or disagreement, such as when two students remember the detail differently. You will also be able to immerse your students in demonstrations of the use of a table of contents, the glossary, headings in text, and bold print in a nonfiction book as opposed to bold print in a fiction book. Many opportunities will present themselves.

Closing Thoughts

Young children request the same book over and over. Ask any parent or grandparent caring for a toddler or a preschooler. Yet, at school, it seems we are in such a rush to get things done that we attempt to unpack all we can pull from a book in one reading. The power of visiting and having several return visits with a book is that it builds on what young children have already shown us. They need time to relish the familiar as they build a context that enables them to examine and notice the nuances that may often be overlooked in our rush to cover.

The Art of the Read-Aloud

"Use beautiful, content-rich, age- and grade-appropriate picture books—short stories or poetry or short informational pieces illustrated with beautiful art— as a foundation for thinking, talking, and writing."

—IRENE FOUNTAS AND GAY SU PINNELL

For just a few moments, try to conjure up an image in your mind of a parent holding a toddler and telling a story. Perhaps the story is "Goldilocks and the Three Bears" or "The Gingerbread Man" or "Little Red Riding Hood." It might even be a simple nursery rhyme such as "Little Miss Muffet." Now that you have the image, lean in and listen to the telling of the story. Listen to the voice of the storyteller and notice the differences in the pitch when Papa Bear speaks and when Mama Bear speaks. Notice how the pacing changes as the tension in the story begins to mount. Listen to the storyteller stretch out words like "great big papa bear bowl" and increase the speed to push words together when the action is fast-paced. Notice as you listen to the shift in the voice when a character is frightened or angry or excited. When we tell stories, it seems almost natural for us to unconsciously attend to the significant role that tone, intensity, pacing, and mood can play in helping the child make sense of the story. It seems natural as a scaffold for comprehension when we are telling our little ones a story. Before you let go of that image, take a look at the face of the storyteller. You probably notice facial expressions and body language and hand gestures that attempt to make the language easier to understand. Each aspect of the storyteller's rendition of the story is a layer to help the child make meaning, to engage the child in the story, and to create a bond between the humans involved.

Indulge me further and conjure a second image. This time, picture an adult reading a book aloud to a small group of children. The group may be siblings, cousins, or friends gathered for a party, a sleepover, or a playdate. The group may be a group of schoolchildren. Let's say the book is a picture book. Now lean in and listen. Do you hear those shifts in pitch to signal a different character is speaking? Do you hear the elongations of selected words being stretched for emphasis? Do you hear the pacing change when the action is mounting? Do you see the reader using facial expressions or hand gestures that match the story? For some reason, these things seem less natural to adults in a read-aloud than in storytelling.

Reading aloud well borrows from the art of storytelling. To present the text with an accurate rendition of the words but without attention to tone, intensity, mood, and pacing is like leaving the icing off the cake. To read aloud without attention to rhythm, pitch, and stress makes the sound of the reading expressionless, less robust, less meaningful, just… less. Whether it's a first visit or a return visit, to read aloud well, the reader, like the storyteller, must attend to at least these four qualities.

HOME VISIT

Introduce Families to the Joy of the Read-Aloud

scholastic.com/URAResources

Invite families to watch Lester explain the most engaging ways to read aloud favorite books to children. A link is provided in the Family Letter that can be downloaded online (or go directly to https://youtu.be/ViNXcEuthF8). You can also share the videos at a Family Literacy Event or Back-to-School Night.

1. TONE. I think of the tone of the text as the attitude of the text. Is it chatty and informal, sincere, snarky, caustic, arrogant, formal and distant, cheerful, solemn, pushing, pleading, preachy, or academic? The writer's attitude and feeling toward the subject will set the tone. Tone may also reflect what the writer intends to make the reader feel. In the read-aloud your voice should reflect the tone of the text.

2. MOOD. I think of the mood of a text as the emotional climate of the piece, its temperament, or the way it leaves the reader feeling. Is it sad, depressed, hopeful, wishful, excited, eager, or nostalgic? Often the setting, voice, and personality of the character will help establish mood. As we reach the end of the reading, the mood should linger like a fragrance.

3. INTENSITY. I think of intensity as the energy of the text. Is it powerful and bold, or tender and quiet? Does the energy build and wane? Or does it launch with a punch and remain at that level? Or does it begin full and slowly dwindle? Perhaps it is quiet and gentle from the first line to the last. The intensity of a piece will be reflected in a read-aloud by the shifts in volume and the power of the reader's voice.

4. PACING. I think of pacing as the heartbeat of the text. It is a pulse, a rhythm that creates the flow of the language. It may race at times and slow to a heart-stopping standstill at others. We feel the effect of pacing when the reader's voice employs a dramatic pause or begins rushing to build tension. We feel the effect when a reader's voice moves as slow as honey on a February morning to draw the listener in. It may be heard and felt when a reader stretches a word for emphasis or runs through words like a babbling brook to reflect the action of the piece.

Reading aloud well is like playing music. As the reader, you are a musician of sorts and your instrument is your voice. Not only must you (the reader) be able to "read" the words with accuracy, you must also be able to interpret the intentions of the writer regarding tone, intensity, pacing, and mood. The texts we read aloud for our students have signals that indicate the intentions of writers (and the team of people who work in layout and design to produce a book), which are in many ways like the signals provided by composers for musicians.

"There's no exact right way of reading aloud, other than to try to be as expressive as possible. As we read a story, we need to be aware of our body posture, our eyes and their expression, our eye contact with the child or children, our vocal variety, and our general facial animation. But each of us will have our own special way of doing it."

—MEM FOX

SPOTLIGHT ON LESTER VIDEO

More on the Art of the Read-Aloud

scholastic.com/URAResources

For example, in music, when a composer intends for the musician to increase or decrease the intensity of the music, this may be signaled by special marks, which look something like an elongated less-than sign (<) for an increase or *crescendo*, or an elongated greater-than sign (>) for a decrease or *decrescendo*. The musician interprets these notations and adjusts the sound or level of intensity when playing. These shifts in intensity not only capture the attention of the listeners, but they also help convey the emotional content of the music.

Composers also indicate their intentions regarding the pacing of a piece with a time signature (3/4, 4/4, etc.) indicating the number of beats in each measure. This sets a pace, or creates a rhythm for the piece. So a series of whole notes, where each measure is a single note being played for four beats, may seem slow and languid to the ear. However, the composer may create a sense of movement by placing two half-notes, getting two beats each in one measure, followed by a measure with four quarter-notes, getting one beat each. And to create a greater sense of urgency, we may find a measure with eighth notes and sixteenth notes. If the composer decides that a span of silence would create a desired effect, that will be signaled by a rest. The use of silence is an important part of music. Silence in well-chosen places draws your attention to the music. The composer can create a feeling or tone with the combination of pacing and intensity.

Readers can find signals regarding intensity and pacing in print as well. Just as composers use visual cues to signal their intentions, writers use punctuation and shifts in font, bold print, underlining and italics, size of print, syllable length, word length and sentence length, line breaks, white space, and more to indicate their intentions regarding intensity in the performance of the text. As a reader, you recognize that a word printed in bold type suggests that you should increase the intensity of your voice. Likewise, when the print becomes gradually smaller, you would let your voice become gradually softer. Intensity may also be signaled with punctuation marks. Every first-grade student clearly understands that an exclamation point signals excitement. Even first graders know that means your voice becomes stronger and louder. If the writer includes more than one exclamation point, all capital letters, bold print, red lettering, and a larger font, you recognize immediately that you are expected to boost the volume and convey some big message. And if you just read right past that, children will stop you in midsentence and point to the writer's signals, letting you know you didn't read that right. As readers, we come to recognize that a question mark at the end of a line signals a shift in intensity and tone. Ellipses indicate that we should let our voices trail off as if there were more to say but it was better left unsaid, or to indicate that there was a word left out deliberately. It is our voices that communicate these purposes to the listener.

"The ups and downs of our voices and our pauses and points of emphasis are like music, literally, to the ears of young children, and kids love music."

—MEM FOX

INSIDE THE BEST FRIEND READ-ALOUD (FICTION)

The Recess Queen, written by Alexis O'Neill and illustrated by Laura Huliska-Beith

Let's explore the signals in a boisterous story of a playground bully. In *The Recess Queen* by Alexis O'Neill, with art by Laura Huliska-Beith, we meet a young girl who is a playground bully.

TONE

The overall tone of this read-aloud is bright, quick, a bit aggressive, with a shift at the end toward friendship.

INTENSITY

Energy runs high in this read-aloud. Your voice will need to reflect the high energy of a playground and translate the emotions at play.

PACING

The pace matches the energy and the quick pulse of moving across a crowded playground.

MOOD

The general mood of this book is humorous, yet the subject is more serious.

The opening lines on the first spread present the bully:

MEAN JEAN was Recess Queen

and nobody said any different.

This first sentence is presented on two lines, again suggesting a particular emphasis. The first line establishes Mean Jean's identity. The second line makes it clear that her identity is unchallenged.

The next page (opposing page on the same spread) presents three sentences that are listed as three separate statements rather than written in paragraph form:

Nobody swung until Mean Jean swung.

Nobody kicked until Mean Jean kicked.

Nobody bounced until Mean Jean bounced.

The language is presented in phrases. Does that suggest a slow, deliberate pace? Not to me. Note that the first two words in the first sentence are in a different font, all capital letters and in bold print—"**MEAN JEAN**." That suggests a strong voice, a bold beginning, as if the composer is signaling the musician to begin with an *ff* (*fortissimo* or very loud). We open with intensity that helps establish the identity of the main character and sets the tone of dominance that a bully works so hard to create. As we continue, the language is presented in a bold, clear, tight font that is unembellished, suggesting to me that we are to keep that tone present as we read.

Let's examine how the presentation of the language actually makes a difference in how we make it sound when we read aloud. By way of contrast, try reading this opening, written in paragraph form, with a more traditional font, and without the use of capital letters at the beginning of the sentence. It would look like this:

Mean Jean was Recess Queen and nobody said any different.

Nobody swung until Mean Jean swung. Nobody kicked until

Mean Jean kicked. Nobody bounced until Mean Jean bounced.

So just read it aloud a few times as if you are reading a paragraph. Of course, if you have read the book aloud many times, you may be influenced by your attention to the features of the print and the presentation of the art. So try to divorce your mind from those influences. Just read the sentences in the paragraph as if you were the anchor on the six o'clock news. . . . It sounds flat, doesn't it? And you certainly don't leave with a highly emotional response to Jean.

Now let's layer the format back into the presentation. I'll change the layout to simulate the presentation in the book:

MEAN JEAN was Recess Queen

and nobody said any different.

Nobody swung until Mean Jean swung.

Nobody kicked until Mean Jean kicked.

Nobody bounced until Mean Jean bounced.

Wow, what a difference that makes! Clearly, this will not sound like the anchor on the six o'clock news. This bold print, the enlarged font, and the line breaks suggest something more for me. Consider the following suggestions. Note how the bold print, the selection of font, and the subject (bullying) lead you toward a sense of defiance, a strong voice, a louder voice:

MEAN JEAN was Recess Queen	[Bold voice to establish her role.]
and nobody said any different.	[Defiant tone, dare anyone to challenge.]

On the next page (opposing page of the same spread), note how the sentences are presented in a list, making the parallel structure quite visible. This creates a listing effect, as if you are making the rules quite clear. It is also introducing the main character and establishing her role as playground bully. That personality is more evident in this presentation:

Nobody swung until Mean Jean swung.	[Bold, defiant voice; full stop.]
Nobody kicked until Mean Jean kicked.	[Bold, defiant voice; full stop.]
Nobody bounced until Mean Jean bounced.	[Bold, defiant voice; full stop.]

When I consider the art, I have even more signals for interpreting the sound of this book. The illustrations are rendered in bold and bright acrylic and collage, giving the book a strong and vivid look. The opening spread makes a clear statement, with Mean Jean consuming practically all of the first page. Her arms are crossed, her body is leaning in toward the center of the page, and her head is the largest feature on the spread. Her face has a snarky, satisfied grimace and her eyes glare across the spread into a crowd of children clustered somewhat like bowling pins. The faces of the children are wide-eyed, with mouths drawn in tight little O's as they await the signal from Mean Jean letting them know they have her permission to play. The bold color, paired with a perspective that presents a sharp contrast between the size of Jean and the other children, creates a defiant, bold, bullying tone that is supported by the features in the print. These features could create an aggressive feel, but are abated somewhat by the animated style of illustration.

WHEN PREPARING FOR A READ-ALOUD EXPERIENCE:

- Consider the artwork: Do the colors suggest a bold, boisterous voice or a quiet, more subdued tone? Is there movement and energy calling for a more rapid pace and greater intensity, or is the art more static and peaceful, calling for a slower, softer voice?

- Read the dedication yourself and share it with your students if there is additional insight offered there—the dedication can offer a window into the author's motives and connections to the text.

- Examine the endpapers—these often carry a motif or design from the text, giving insight into a theme or feeling for the book that can influence your presentation of the language.

- Consider the genre and what you know and expect from texts written in that genre—a biography would be read with different emphasis than humor or poetry, for example.

- Review the author and illustrator information on the flap—this information can provide insight into the influences in the writing or illustration style, topic, and presentation.

- Preview the book by reading it aloud to yourself ahead of time; listen for the rhythm and find the flow.

- Read the book at least once silently, and then once aloud to find the rhythm, and note the points in the text where you might need to pause or quicken the pace, drop your voice to a whisper, or build to a near shout.

- Note those places in the text where you may need to pause for a brief comment or scaffold meaning for the audience—avoid overdoing this, and be careful to recognize that it isn't necessary in every book.

- Change the tone of your voice to match the dialogue or the personality of the characters, or to set the mood when possible.

- Adjust your pace to fit the story, slowing down for dramatic pauses and speeding up to create movement and energy.

- Make your voice expressive; convey the emotional quality of the text.

- Know why you are presenting a particular text; be clear about your expectations of the book, your presentation, and the students—let this information guide your voice as it conveys tone and mood through pacing and intensity.

- Position yourself so that both you and the children are comfortable, your voice can carry to the entire group, and the illustrations (if there are any) can be seen.

- Vary the length and subject matter of the read-aloud experience. Include picture books, storybooks, chapter books, nonfiction, and poetry.

- Allow your listeners a few minutes to settle down and adjust their bodies and minds to the story.

- Allow time for (but don't require) discussion after reading.

- Add a third dimension to the book when it will add depth and enhance the experience—for example, bring a bowl of blueberries to be eaten after reading Robert McCloskey's *Blueberries for Sal*.

> *"Powerful writers and powerful speakers have two wells they can draw on for that power: one is the well of rhythm; the other is the well of vocabulary. But vocabulary and a sense of rhythm are almost impossible to 'teach' in the narrow sense of the word. So how are children to develop a sense of rhythm or a wide vocabulary? By being read to, aloud, a lot!"*
>
> **—MEM FOX**

INSIDE THE BEST FRIEND
READ-ALOUD (NONFICTION)

Polar Bears, written and illustrated by Gail Gibbons

TONE

The overall tone of this read-aloud is sober, solemn, and focused.

INTENSITY

The energy of this text is steady and controlled, and should favor the information over the presentation.

PACING

The general pace of this read-aloud is rather consistent. There are a few places where the pace would slow a bit to give the listeners time to process the information.

MOOD

The general mood of this read-aloud is serious, informative.

By now you may be wondering how this might be different with a nonfiction text. Let's take a look at *Polar Bears* by Gail Gibbons. The first thing I notice with this book is the author's name. I have come to trust Gail Gibbons to deliver a detailed, factual presentation of information in a concise and accessible style. True to form, when I open this book, I find large illustrations that are realistic (not like photographs, but not animated or cartoon-like, either). A quick look through the book reveals the use of captions and labels with many of the illustrations. Take a moment to read the text on any page where these captions or labels are included in the art, and you find that they illuminate the information or expand the role of the text. In short, this book is meant to teach us something about polar bears. It isn't a story about a polar bear's day or a story in which a polar bear is a character. Instead, it is solid information.

When I step into an information book, my mind turns on the voice of the Discovery Channel narrators. I hear that careful and deliberate pace that avoids rushing an idea. I hear the clear and articulate voice enunciating carefully with a focus on the information over all else. I hear the timbre of a voice of authority, a voice I should trust. And as I open a Gail Gibbons book, I hear that same voice. The tone is more formal and serious, suggesting an intensity that is powerful yet restrained, with a pace that is careful and deliberate, pausing intentionally in places for my mind to catch up with the flow of the information.

POLAR BEAR

The snow blows, the wind howls. The temperature is very cold, hovering around −30 degrees Fahrenheit (−34 degrees Celsius). Through the snowy scene a great white bear appears, the polar bear.

Let's take a closer look at the opening page:

> **The snow blows, the wind howls. The temperature is very cold, hovering around −30 degrees Fahrenheit (−34 degrees Celsius).**
>
> **Through the snowy scene a great white bear appears, the polar bear.**

Can't you hear that voice? Hold that voice in your head and read through these opening lines. Here's what I hear:

> **"The snow blows,**   [Pause and hold the *s* on *blows* for a second.]

the wind	[Place a slight emphasis on the *d* in *wind*, creating the slightest pause.]
howls.	[Full stop.]
The temperature is very	[Emphasis on *very*.]
cold,	[Slight emphasis on the *d* in *cold*, creating a very slight pause.]
hovering around −30 degrees Fahrenheit	[Pause here and drop your voice before *degrees Fahrenheit*.]
(−34 degrees Celsius).	[The lower voice suggests an aside, like saying "in other words."]
Through the snowy scene	[Carefully enunciate these two words—*snowy/scene*.]
a great white bear	[Place a slight emphasis on these words—*great/white/bear*.]
appears,	[Pause and alter the intensity as if you are announcing the arrival of someone.]
the polar bear.	

Let's take a look at another small sample and notice how control of pacing and intensity can help call attention to vocabulary. In this passage, the word *tundra* is defined by the words preceding it:

The polar bear lives in the Arctic, the area that surrounds the North Pole. Part of the Arctic is frozen, treeless land called tundra. Most of the Arctic is ocean. Ice covers the water most of the year.

In some of the fiction we examined earlier, we took signals for pacing and intensity from the placement of words on the page and/or from the use of white spaces. In this book and many nonfiction books we find a more typical paragraph structure, which provides no signals about pacing or intensity. So we take our cues from the language and the layering of ideas. Let's play with pacing and intensity here and find out how they can influence the power of the language. Read the three sentences above and try to keep your pace steady, in a low, quiet volume. Now try that aloud one or two times. Notice how doing so has you move right over the word *tundra* and how the definition could get lost by the time you reach the end of the fourth sentence.

Notice that these four sentences are focused on the habitat of polar bears. The four sentences are building that one big idea, yet that one big idea is made up of these six smaller ideas:

1. **Polar bears live in the Arctic.**

2. **The Arctic is the area surrounding the North Pole.**

3. **Part of the Arctic is frozen, treeless land.**

4. **That frozen, treeless land is called tundra.**

5. **Most of the Arctic is ocean.**

6. **Ice covers the water most of the year.**

Now try it again with that Discovery Channel narrator voice in your head. Think about how we placed emphasis on key words and particular sounds to draw attention to those ideas. Think about how we paused in targeted places to give the mind a chance to layer in the ideas that are building across the sentences. Try reading aloud with attention to pacing and intensity that will help the audience layer the six smaller ideas to gain insight into the one big idea.

Let's take one sentence from the four: "Part of the Arctic is frozen, treeless land called tundra." Note how the sentence embeds a definition for new vocabulary (*tundra*). To read this too quickly would likely result in the audience whizzing right past that connection. And they are just as likely to miss the notion that only part of the Arctic is tundra. So let's try to control pacing and intensity in a way that would call attention to those two ideas.

"Part	[Place emphasis on this word.]
of the Arctic	[Slight pause.]
is frozen, treeless land	[Slight pause.]
called tundra."	[Emphasize the word *tundra*.]

Do you hear a difference this way? The shift in intensity to stress the words *part* and *tundra* calls attention to them, gives them weight. The pauses or attention to pacing help the listener layer information and build meaning. The simple act of attending to tone, intensity, pacing, and mood can make every read-aloud more robust.

INSIDE THE BEST FRIEND READ-ALOUD (FICTION)

Snow Day! written by Lester L. Laminack and illustrated by Adam Gustavson

Intensity in the read-aloud can be examined with *Snow Day!* by Lester L. Laminack. This book (yes, I wrote it) is a story of anticipation—living through those hours between the weatherman's prediction for significant snowfall and the morning after. The intensity or energy in this book is evident from the first line and continues at a high level to the last line.

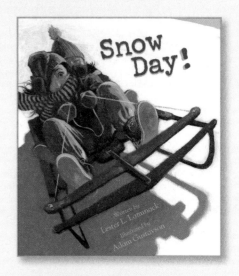

TONE

The overall tone of this read-aloud is jovial, fun.

INTENSITY

Energy begins high and remains high.

PACING

Overall, the pace of this read-aloud is rather steady. It moves at a quick clip that reflects the high energy of the text.

SPOTLIGHT ON LESTER VIDEO

Lester Reads *Snow Day!* by Lester L. Laminack

scholastic.com/URAResources

MOOD

The general mood of this book is eager anticipation, leaving the reader with a positive, upbeat feeling.

Let's step inside:

Did you *hear* that?

Did the weatherman just say what I

thought he did?

Did he say...

SNOW?

Oh please, let it snow. Lots and lots of snow.

First notice the short sentences dancing back and forth on the page. Notice the word *snow* popping out at you. This is the announcement that snow is on the way. That builds energy and anticipation in most households with school-age children (or at least one teacher). That energy calls for intensity in your voice when you read aloud.

Imagine reading this aloud to your students as if you were that six o'clock news anchor:

Did you hear that? Did that weatherman just say what I thought he did? Did he say . . . SNOW? Oh please, let it snow. Lots and lots of snow.

Even this presentation of the print zaps energy from this much-anticipated event. Consider it again in the original form:

Did you *hear* that?

[The narrator is speaking directly to you. Notice the italics used for emphasis, nudging you to punch up the intensity there.]

Did the weatherman just say what I thought he did?

[Notice the space between the first line and this one, signaling you to pause. It's as if you are waiting to hear from the weatherman again. Your voice calls to the listener to confirm what you heard, engaging the audience.]

Did he say . . .

[Notice the hesitation, the trailing off marked by the ellipses.]

SNOW?

[How could you miss this cue? Notice the enlarged font, the use of all capitals, and bold print begging you to significantly increase the intensity.]

Oh please, let it snow.
Lots and lots of snow.

[This is a plea. Let your voice plead with the audience.]

In this presentation, the placement of text, the use of font size and italics and bold, the series of three questions, and a plea all work together to build the energy of a possible snowfall and the hope for a snow day. So when you read it aloud, the intensity of your voice should reflect that energy, leaving the audience with that sense of eager anticipation.

MY FAVORITE WAYS TO INTRODUCE A BOOK

1. PICTURE WALK

2. BOOK TALK/COMMERCIAL

3. AUTHOR PROFILE

4. THEME/TOPIC LINK

5. JUST START READING

Picture Walk

Today we are going to read this book [hold the book so the front cover is visible]. *It is called* Snow Day! *The author is Lester Laminack, and the illustrator is Adam Gustavson. Take a look at the illustration on the front. These two kids seem to be zipping down a hill on this red sled. Before we read this one, let's take a walk through the pictures and see what is going on.* [Turn to the first illustration and begin a conversation. It may go something like what follows]: *Well, I see a boy looking right at us and his eyes are really large. He looks excited. I wonder what he might be excited about. And look at the girl lying there on the floor in front of the TV. Mmmm, that's interesting, the man on the TV is standing in front of a map and that looks like clouds and snowflakes. I wonder what that man is talking about. Oh look, there is one more person in the illustration. See the man over here? He looks like a grown-up, and he's wearing an apron and has a spatula in his hand. It looks as if he is coming from the kitchen to see what is going on. Now I'm really wondering what these three are talking about. Let's turn the page and take a look at the next illustration, shall we?*

HOME VISIT

Help Students Introduce Best Friend Books to Families
scholastic.com/URAResources

At school, students learned multiple ways to introduce a Best Friend Book. Now invite them to introduce their BFBs to their families. Consider making videos of students introducing their Best Friend Books to share at home.

Book Talk/Commercial

*Just imagine how excited you'd feel if you heard the TV weatherperson
announce the possibility of a big snowfall on a SCHOOL NIGHT! Imagine what
you'd be thinking about and how excited you would get. Perhaps you'd be thinking
about staying up late to watch TV. Or sleeping in the next morning. Or you might
be thinking about your homework and how you could just skip it until the next day.
Maybe you'd be thinking about all the fun you could have spending the day playing
in the snow—snow forts and snowball fights, sledding and snowmen. . . . Oh, and
then you'd need to come inside and get warm. There's bound to be hot chocolate
on a snow day—mmmm, I do love a good mug full of hot chocolate. Today we are
reading* Snow Day! *I can hardly wait, let's get right to it and see what happens on
this snow day. . . .*

Author Profile

Today I have a new book for us. This one is called Snow Day!, *and look, it's written
by Lester Laminack. We know who that is. He wrote* Saturdays and Teacakes. *He
also wrote other books that we have in our classroom library; do you remember
which books he wrote? Let's take a look [have the books close by and hold each one
up]. He wrote* Jake's 100th Day of School *and* Trevor's Wiggly-Wobbly Tooth. *Those
stories remind us of the things we do at school. We have talked about that several
times. He also wrote* The Sunsets of Miss Olivia Wiggins; *remember how that one
always makes me cry because it reminds me of my grandmother? He wrote one of
our favorites,* Three Hens and a Peacock, *and he also wrote* The King of Bees. *Do
you remember how that book got us so excited about honeybees that we decided
to do a study of honeybees? I checked Lester's website and bookmarked the page
for you if you'd like to go there for yourself. I discovered that Lester was
a teacher in an elementary school and in a university. That helps us understand
why he might write about what happens at school in* Trevor's Wiggly-Wobbly Tooth
and Jake's 100th Day of School. *I'm thinking* Snow Day! *might have a connection
to school as well. Let's try to remember to look for that as we read. I also found
out that he grew up in a very small Alabama town called Heflin. And I discovered
that* Saturdays and Teacakes *is a memoir about growing up in that small town. I
am wondering if there is anything from his life in this book,* Snow Day! *Let's think
about that when we are listening. Remind me to check the dedication, since authors
sometimes share connections for us there. And one more thing I discovered when
reading about Lester. He lives in Whittier, North Carolina. I wonder if it snows there.
Maybe that is how he got the idea for this book. Let's take a look inside and see
what we find.*

Theme/Topic Link

Sometimes unexpected things can make us change our plans. Rainstorms can cause us to cancel soccer practice. A flat tire on a bike can make us walk when we planned to ride. Sometimes we expect something in the mail and it takes a week longer to arrive than we thought it would. A delay at the airport can cause us to miss a trip. Unexpected events can make us change our plans, and that is what we are reading about this week. I have a basket of books here, and we will read one each day. These are stories about all kinds of plans that just don't work out because something unexpected happens. Let's take a look at the first one, Snow Day!, *written by Lester Laminack with illustrations by Adam Gustavson. Take a moment before we begin to read; let's think about what unexpected event may make these characters change their plans. What plans do you suppose they had?* [At this point, I sometimes have students share their thinking with someone nearby first, then share out.] *Let's settle in and see what goes awry in this story. . . .*

Just Start Reading

Well, duh . . . this is pretty clear, huh? All kidding aside, I often just share the title, author, and illustrator, then begin.

Stepping Back to Consider Our Intentions

When you next launch a read-aloud experience in your classroom, think about your intentions. Are you reading aloud to *inspire* your students to become readers and writers? Are you trying to have them fall in love with a genre, topic, title, author, or illustrator? Or is the experience an *investment* in the development of their language and understanding? Are you building background for future instruction? Or will you be reading aloud to them at the point of *instruction*? Will you select the text you read for the purpose of teaching them something? Will this text build off the previous ones? Will it be grounded in a unit of study in a subject area?

Whatever your intentions when you next read aloud, think about setting the stage to maximize the effect. Our students thrive on structure and routine, so the read-aloud experience should be a consistent event. You can find very specific suggestions for six opportunities for reading aloud across a single day in *Learning Under the Influence of Language and Literature* (Laminack & Wadsworth, 2006). In that book, Reba Wadsworth and I suggest six different times in the typical school day when teachers might insert a read-aloud. In addition, we offer a very specific purpose for each of them. You will also find more than 400 picture books listed out, annotated, and organized by purpose. Having a designated time and purpose is important. It is also important to set the stage in other ways.

- **Physical setting**—have a consistent location from which you will read. If the audience is seated in chairs, I like sitting on a tall stool while reading aloud. Otherwise, I prefer to sit on the floor, with my audience gathered close enough to see the illustrations.

- **Select a location that makes the book visible** without having the glare of a window behind you, and avoid sitting in a position that causes the audience to have to look up the entire time.

- **Establish an atmosphere in the classroom that supports engagement** in the read-aloud experience. Clear other materials and work away. Make yourself and the text the focal point. Eliminate distractions or reduce them to a minimum.

- **Introduce the text you are presenting in the read-aloud**—show the cover and announce the title, author, and illustrator. Invite the students to examine the cover art. Read the flap copy regarding the text and the brief profile of the author and illustrator. Read the dedication. Examine the endpapers and do a brief picture walk through the text to get an overview, become familiar with the layout, and make note of text features in nonfiction. Lead the students to use the information garnered to make predictions about the text.

- **Introduce the read-aloud experience by stating your purpose:** "Today as I read I'd like you to be thinking about . . . ," or "I selected this text for read-aloud today because it will help us understand what was going on during the days when Anne Frank was a little girl. . . ."

- **If your intentions for the read-aloud experience warrant it, draw attention to specific features of the text,** such as text boxes, charts, sidebars, graphs, captions, labels, bold type, font type shifts, font size shifts, diagrams, the index, appendices, and so on.

- **If your intentions warrant it, pause at critical junctures** to raise questions in students' minds.

WHAT THE RESEARCH SAYS

Wasik and Bond (2001) investigated the learning potential of the interactive read-aloud. Their study, which included 121 four-year-old children from low-income families (94 percent of whom were African American), engaged the treatment group in interactive book reading. This included defining vocabulary words, providing opportunities for children to use words from the books, asking open-ended questions, and giving children a chance to talk and be heard. The control teachers received all the books that the treatment teachers did and read the books as often in their control classrooms as the treatment teachers read in their classrooms; however, control teachers did not receive the interactive read-aloud training that treatment teachers received.

For the first four weeks of the intervention, an experienced teacher modeled the interactive book reading techniques in each treatment classroom. Then, for the next 11 weeks, treatment teachers ran the program on their own. At post-test, treatment classes scored significantly higher on the Peabody Picture Vocabulary than control classes did. Treatment classes also scored significantly higher on their knowledge of target vocabulary words, perhaps in part because treatment teachers were significantly more likely to use the target words during related activities.

Closing Thoughts

Read-alouds, when done well, are like a storytelling performance. The reader must take the time necessary to preview and rehearse the book, just as a storyteller would. The voice is the instrument that brings life to the language of the writer, and that voice has to convey the tone of the characters and the narrator, the emotion of the scene, and the mood of the situation. We cannot reasonably expect that our students will hear those features of a story in their own minds unless we provide a demonstration for what is possible. We are the models for how fluency works—how written language flows into sound with the potential to lift meaning. We set examples for how a character's personality influences tone, and how emotions influence intensity. We demonstrate how the voice conveys mood. When reading nonfiction aloud, think of the narrator voices you have heard in documentary films. The voice is steady; inflection varies, but less so than in fiction. Pacing takes on significance because there are layers of information presented. The reader pauses to let the information sink in as the author transitions between topics. The tone is usually more serious. Reading aloud is no frivolous activity; it is solid instructional work when our intentions are clear.

HOME VISIT

**Help Families Understand What a BFB Collection Is
and How to Create Their Own**
scholastic.com/URAResources

Invite families to watch Lester explain what a Best Friend Book Collection is, how to create one at home, and ways to use it on a regular, joyful basis. A link is provided in the Family Letter that can be downloaded online (or go directly to https://youtu.be/Ao9G4Jd1CEo). You can also share the video at a Family Literacy Event or Back-to-School Night.

Closing Comments and a Final Plea

"From that day forward, words and sentences and books, I discovered, when read and recited, could heal a tender heart."

—JUAN FELIPE HERRERA, POET LAUREATE, 2015–2017

Most of us have had the experience of watching the same movie a second (or third) time. Most of us have viewed and viewed again (and perhaps again) the same episode of a favorite show on television. Even though we know what is going to happen, we watch again. We laugh again. We cry again. We are moved again. All of us have listened so often to a favorite song that we know the lyrics and sing along; perhaps we even sing in the shower without the music to accompany us.

When a story resonates with our hearts and minds, there is an inexplicable pull. The text (book, poem, article, movie, television program, song) lingers with us and we are drawn back to it. We need time to take it in because one visit didn't leave us satisfied. So we visit again, and perhaps again and again. There is something comforting about relishing the familiar that sets us up to notice the nuances we missed in first or second visits.

So it shouldn't surprise us that children want, if not need, the opportunity to visit with some stories again and again. Let us honor that need to get to know a few books intimately and hold them in our hearts and minds. Time spent reading aloud to children is never wasted. Let us slow the pace to unearth the nuances in language and art, in the actions and reactions of familiar characters, in the craft and technique and style of favorite authors, in the dialogue and narration of selected stories, in the transition between selected topics, and when the writer artfully layers in topic-specific vocabulary and deftly defines it in context.

Yes, I said let us slow the pace. I know the pressures are real—to do more, to cover more material, to push harder, and to do it all more quickly. I know the call to raise scores and achieve more. But we cannot lose sight of this truth: We are working with children. Honor the learner. Relish the learning. We are cultivating the hearts and minds of those who will lead this world in the years of our retirement. We are raising humans.

WHAT THE RESEARCH SAYS

Anne Cunningham, renowned cognitive psychologist at the University of California, Berkeley, explains that reading is a "very rich, complex, and cognitive act" that offers an immense opportunity to exercise our intelligence in ways we lose if we don't read. Hundreds of correlated studies demonstrate that the most successful students read the most, while those who struggle read the least. These correlated studies suggest that the more our students read, the better their comprehension, vocabulary, and fluency—and the more likely they are to build a robust knowledge of the world. In short, reading provides us with a cognitive workout that transcends not only our inherent abstract problem-solving abilities, but also our levels of education. Reading makes us smart. (Cunningham & Zibulsky, 2014)

Humans need story. Story is how we make sense of our lives. Story helps us make sense of yesterday, navigate today, and imagine tomorrow. Story lets us see ourselves in a world larger than we can imagine on our own. Story lets us see others as a part of this one shared world, as members of this one human family. Story lets us imagine more. Story gives us a context, a frame of reference for considering the "what ifs" and "why nots" in life. Story helps us to be more, to outgrow our current selves, and to see beyond the horizon of our current circumstances. Story is essential to our existence.

It doesn't take much for us to imagine the benefits of having five thoughtfully selected stories and five carefully selected nonfiction titles in a classroom that become treasures in the hearts and minds of every single student. The investment

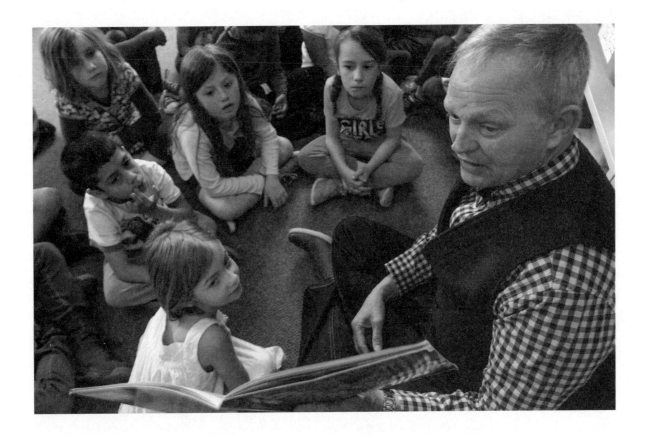

of time to slow down and introduce each of the five books as new best friends is negligible. Those first visits are gifts of time, gifts of story, gifts of information and language, gifts of heart. And children know when a gift is given with a joyful heart. Knowing that you will visit again and again with a small collection of books removes the pressure to "strip mine" a beautiful story. Slowing down does not mean doing less. Rather, it means being more intentional, more focused, and more thoughtful about what you want your reader/writers to embrace and carry forward into their literate lives. Just imagine that while you confer with the readers and writers in your classroom, you know that each of them holds those same five fiction and five nonfiction texts in their hearts and heads. You know that you can refer to any scene in any of the ten texts, and each child will hold that reference in mind. Reading and writing with that knowledge and enhanced vocabulary "on deposit" puts us in a place where conversations about personal reading and writing share common connectors across the classroom community. So we read aloud. We read aloud with the zeal of a street performer and with the frequency of bird song. We read aloud knowing it matters. We read aloud with clear intentions and with focused instructional goals.

WHAT THE RESEARCH SAYS

The tangible rewards of reading aloud and discussing books with our children are both extensive and well grounded in research. Indeed, in 1985, the federally funded Commission on Reading released a report entitled "Becoming a Nation of Readers" that stated: "The single most important activity for building the knowledge required for eventual success is reading aloud to children." (1985, p. 23)

See also:

Johnson, A. (2018). In D. Miller and C. Sharp, (eds.) *Game-Changer! Book Access for All Kids*. New York: Scholastic.

Scharer, P. (2018). *Responsive Literacy: The Comprehensive Framework*. New York: Scholastic.

Bringing books into the community as new best friends operates on the assumption that we know those books intimately ourselves. It assumes we have read and reread those stories again and again, each time with a particular focus in mind. In other words, we have given ourselves the same experience that we are planning for our students because we understand that we cannot lead them where we have not traveled ourselves.

Take some time now to search through your books, to carefully and critically examine your schedule, to revisit your vision about why this matters. Pull a favorite book, stop what you are doing, and read to them.

Take time to read and reread the books in your collection to find those you can introduce as Best Friend Books. Slow down; give your students the pleasure of meeting a new character, exploring a new setting, facing a new challenge, or delving into intriguing information, text features, or topic vocabulary as you introduce them to your best friends. Slow down; take the time to let that first meeting be a gift you unwrap together without interruption. Know that you will revisit these friends again and again as you build deep and abiding relationships between your students and the love of language, story, information, and the written word.

Friends, I urge you to reconnect to those stirrings that brought you into this profession. I urge you to refocus your attention to the children in your care. There is no more precious treasure in this world than the children of its people. Nothing holds greater potential for good, for truth, for justice than the children on this Earth.

In all things, be kind and truthful. Let nothing you do take from a child his or her dignity as a human being, his or her integrity as a learner, his or her identity as one who is capable. Cause no intentional harm.

Peace be with you.

> "*When we read great books with our children, we teach them to turn to great books throughout their lives for comfort, humor, and for illumination of the human experience. The most influential leaders and thinkers in the world have consistently relied on literature for inspiration at their most difficult moments.*"
>
> **—KYLE ZIMMER,
> DIRECTOR OF FIRST BOOK**

References

Professional Resources

Allyn, P., & Morrell, E. (2016). *Every child a super reader: 7 strengths to open a world of possible*. New York: Scholastic.

Beck, I. L., & McKeown, M. G. (2001). Text talk: Capturing the benefits of read-aloud experiences for young children. *The Reading Teacher, 55*(1), 10–20.

Beck, I. L., & Sandora, C., (2016). *Illuminating comprehension in close reading*. New York: Guilford Press.

Beers, K., & Probst, R. (2012). *Notice & note: Strategies for close reading*. Portsmouth, NH: Heinemann.

Beers, K., & Probst, R. (2017). *Disrupting thinking: Why how we read matters*. New York: Scholastic.

Commission on Reading. (1985). Becoming a nation of readers. National Institute of Education, Washington, D.C.

Cunningham, A. E., & Zibulsky, J. (2014). *Book smart: How to develop and support successful, motivated readers*. New York: Oxford University Press.

Djikic, M., Oatley, K., & Moldoveanu, M. (2013). "Reading other minds: Effects of literature on empathy." *Scientific Study of Literature*. Vol. 3(1)

Duke, N. (2014). *Inside information: Developing powerful readers and writers of informational text through project-based instruction*. New York: Scholastic.

Duke, N., Caughlan, S., Juzwik, M., & Martin, N. (2012). *Reading and writing genre with purpose in K–8 classrooms* (p. 5). Portsmouth, NH: Heinemann.

Duke, N., Pearson, D., Strachan, S., & Billman, A. (2011). "Essential elements of fostering and teaching reading comprehension." In J. Samuels & A. Farstrup (Eds.), What research has to say about reading instruction (fourth edition). Newark, DE: International Reading Association. Retrieved from:

https://www.readinghalloffame.org/sites/default/files/03-duke-pearson-strachan-billman.2011_rev_copy.pdf

Fountas, I., & Pinnell, G. S. (2006) *Comprehending & fluency*. Portsmouth, NH: Heinemann.

Fountas, I., & Pinnell, G. S. (2017). *Guided reading: Responsive teaching across the grades* (2nd ed.). Portsmouth, NH: Heinemann.

Fox, M. (1993). *Radical reflections*. San Diego, CA: Harcourt.

Fox, M. (2001). *Reading magic*. San Diego, CA: Harcourt.

Halliday, M. A. K. (1973). *Explorations in the functions of language*. London: Edward Arnold.

Harvey, S., & Ward, A. (2017). *From striving to thriving: How to grow confident, capable readers*. New York: Scholastic.

Johnston, P. (2009). Afterword in Nichols, M., *Expanding comprehension with multigenre text sets*. New York: Scholastic.

Kintsch, W., & Rawson, K. A. (2005). Comprehension. In M. J. S. C. Hulme (Ed.), *The science of reading: a handbook*. Malden, MA: Blackwell Publishing (pp. 209–226).

Kittle, P. (in press).

Krashen, S. (2004). *The power of reading* (second edition). Portsmouth, NH: Heinemann Publishing Company, and Westview, CT: Libraries Unlimited.

Krashen, S. (2015). The great fiction/nonfiction debate. *Language Magazine*, November.

Laman, T. T., & Alexander, A. G. (2019). In Stephens, D., Harste, J., Clyde, J. A., Editors. *Reading revealed: 50 expert teachers share what they do and why*. New York: Scholastic.

Laminack, L. L., & Wadsworth, R. M. (2006). *Learning under the influence of language and literature*. Portsmouth, NH: Heinemann.

Laminack, L. L., & Wadsworth, R. M. (2006). *Reading aloud across the curriculum*. Portsmouth, NH: Heinemann.

Laminack, L. L., & Wadsworth, R. M. (2015). *Writers are readers*. Portsmouth, NH: Heinemann.

Miller, D., & Sharp, C. (2018). *Game changer! Book access for all kids*. New York: Scholastic.

Pappano, L. (2015, February 4). Is your first grader college ready? *New York Times*. Retrieved from: http://www.nytimes.com/2015/02/08/education/edlife/is-your-first-grader-college-ready.html

Rasinski, T. (2010). *The fluent reader* (second edition). New York, Scholastic.

Roskos, K., & Neuman, S. (2014, April). Best practices in reading instruction: A 21st century skill update. *The Reading Teacher, 67*(7), 507–511.

Samuels, J. (1979, January). The method of repeated rereadings. *The Reading Teacher, 32*(4) 403–408.

Scharer, P., Editor. (2018). *Responsive literacy: The comprehensive framework*. New York: Scholastic.

Serafini, F. (2008). *Position statement: The vital role of picture books in the intermediate, middle and high school reading curriculum*.

Shefelbine, J., & Newman, K. K. (2004). *Sipps challenge assessment record book*. Oakland, CA: Developmental Studies Center.

Smith, F. (2004). *Understanding reading: A psycholinguistic analysis of reading and learning to read* (6th ed.). New York: Routledge Education.

Stephens, D., Harste, J., & Clyde, J. (2019). *Reading revealed: 50 expert teachers share what they do and why*. New York: Scholastic.

Walther, M. (2018). *The ramped-up read aloud: What to notice as you turn the page*. Thousand Oaks, CA: Corwin.

Wasik, B., & Bond, M. (2001). "The effects of a language and literacy intervention on Head Start children and teachers." Cited in Wasik, B., Bond, M., & Hindman, A. (Feb. 2006). *Journal of Educational Psychology, Vol. 98*(1), 63–74.

Children's Books

Ada, A. F. (2001). *Yours truly, Goldilocks*. New York: Aladdin.

Ada, A. F. (2004). *With love, Little Red Hen*. New York: Aladdin.

Ada, A. F. (2006). *Dear Peter Rabbit*. New York: Aladdin.

Allen, J., & Humphries, T. (2000). *Are you a bee?* New York: Kingfisher.

Ashley, S. (2004). *Bees*. New York: Weekly Reader.

Aston, D. H. (2011). *A butterfly is patient*. (Chronicle Books). New York: Scholastic.

Carney, E. (2009). *Mummies*. (National Geographic Kids). New York: Scholastic.

Dahl, R. (1998). *The BFG*. New York: Puffin Books.

DK. (2016). *The bee book*. London: DK.

Esbaum, J. (2017). *Honey bees*. (National Geographic Kids). New York: Scholastic.

Gibbons, G. (1997). *The honey makers*. New York: HarperCollins.

Gibbons, G. (2002). *Polar bears*. New York: Holiday House.

Gibbons, G. (2007). *Snakes*. New York: Holiday House.

Hall, K. (2018). *The honeybee*. New York: Atheneum.

Henkes, K. (1987). *Sheila Rae the brave*. (Greenwillow Books). New York: Scholastic.

Henkes, K. (1993). *Owen*. (Greenwillow Books). New York: Scholastic.

High, L. O. (1998). *Beekeepers*. Honesdale, PA: Boyds Mills Press.

Huber, R. (2013). *Flight of the honey bee*. Somerville, MA: Candlewick.

Keating, J. (2017). *Shark lady: The true story of how Eugenie Clark became the ocean's most fearless scientist*. (Sourcebooks Jabberwocky). New York: Scholastic.

Keats, E. J. (1998). *A letter to Amy*. New York: Puffin Books.

Keats, E. J. (1998). *Peter's chair*. New York: Puffin Books.

Keats, E. J. (1999). *Apt. 3*. New York: Puffin Books.

Laminack, L. L. (1998). *The sunsets of Miss Olivia Wiggins*. Atlanta: Peachtree.

Laminack, L. L. (1998). *Trevor's wiggly-wobbly tooth*. Atlanta: Peachtree.

Laminack, L. L. (2004). *Saturdays and teacakes*. Atlanta: Peachtree.

Laminack, L. L. (2006). *Jake's 100th day of school*. Atlanta: Peachtree.

Laminack, L. L. (2007). *Snow day!* Atlanta: Peachtree.

Laminack, L. L. (2014). *Three hens and a peacock*. Atlanta: Peachtree.

Laminack, L. L. (2018). *The king of bees*. Atlanta: Peachtree.

Lester, H. (2002). *Hooway for Wodney Wat*. Boston: Walter Lorraine Books.

Lowry, L. (2009). *Crow Call*. New York: Scholastic Press.

McLerran, A. (2004). *Roxaboxen*. New York: HarperTrophy.

Oatman High, L. (1998). *Beekeepers*. Honesdale, PA: Boyds Mills Press.

O'Neill, A. (2002). *The recess queen*. New York: Scholastic.

O'Toole, C. (2013). *Bees: A natural history*. Buffalo, NY: Firefly Books.

Polacco, P. (1998). *The bee tree*. New York: The Putnam Berkley Group.

Rake, M. (2016). *Real-life monsters: Scaly, slippery creatures*. (Lerner Publishing Group). New York: Scholastic.

Rankin, L. (1991). *The handmade alphabet*. New York: Dial Books.

Reynolds, P. H. (2004). *Ish*. Cambridge, MA: Candlewick.

Rockwell, A. (2005). *Honey in a hive*. New York: HarperCollins.

Siebert, D. (2001). *Mississippi*. New York: HarperCollins.

Slade, S. (2011). *What if there were no bees?* Mankato, MN: Picture Window Books.

Stewart, M. (2014). *Zoom in on bees*. Berkeley Heights, NJ: Enslow Publishers.

Teckentrup, B. (2016). *Bee: A peek-through picture book*. London: Little Tiger Press.

TIME for Kids Eds. with E. Winchester. (2005). *Bees!* New York: HarperCollins.

Turner, P. S. (2009). *Prowling the deep: Exploring the hidden world of ocean predators*. New York: Walker & Co.

Wells, R. (1997). *Bunny cakes*. New York: Dial Books for Young Readers.

Index

SCHOLASTICEDUCATION

Meet Every Student's Literacy Goals with

Best-Selling Books and Resources from
Leading Literacy Experts

From foundational skills and fluency to guided and independent reading and writing, we help deepen your practice and facilitate conversations about teaching, learning, equity, and literacy achievement.

Jan Richardson

Kylene Beers & Robert E. Probst

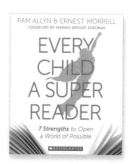
Pam Allyn & Ernest Morrell

Lester L. Laminack

Karen L. Mapp, Ilene Carver, & Jessica Lander

Stephanie Harvey & Annie Ward

Donalyn Miller & Colby Sharp

Rosemarye Taylor & Carol Chanter

Follow our authors
@ScholasticTeach

SCHOLASTIC